Why Did Santa Leave a Body?

WHY DID SANTA LEAVE A BODY?

YULETIDE TALES OF MURDER AND MAYHEM

STORIES BY:

Jessie Chandler
Michael Allan Mallory
Brian Landon
Camille Hyytinen
Barbara DaCosta
Joan Murphy Pride
Dennis Anderson
Kathleen Lindstrom
J. Henry
T.J. Roth
Marlene Chabot

WITH AN INTRODUCTION BY THE EDITOR

Brian Landon

Cover art: Jeffrey Holmes
Title: Douglas Ernst
Contributing Editors: Jessie Chandler, Joan Murphy Pride, T.J. Roth

ISBN-13: 978-1-7335854-6-0

Printed in the United States of America

Published by
Wrong Turn Books
Blaine, Minnesota

Table of Contents

INTRODUCTION BY THE EDITOR

W.C. FIELDS ONCE SAID, "Christmas at my house is always at least six or seven times more pleasant than anywhere else. We start drinking early. And while everyone else is seeing only one Santa Claus, we'll be seeing six or seven."

Fortunately for you, Holly Jolly Reader, we have at least six or seven Santas in store. And you needn't drink to appreciate them (although I find this anthology goes quite well with a glass of egg nog with just a hint of cinnamon). That being said, be forewarned that the Santas contained herein did not spring from a Norman Rockwell painting. Nor was Santa the only target in the sights of the eleven authors who contributed stories to this anthology.

Family members, girlfriends, bosses, and neighbors are all victims on this, the holiest time of year. So put on your fuzzy slippers, wrap up in a cozy blanket, lock the front door, and keep your Smith & Wesson by your side. After all, this isn't just Christmas. This is Christmas in Minnesota – the land of 10,000 mystery writers.

Season's Readings!

Brian Landon
Christmas, 2010

SILENT NIGHT, DEADLY NIGHT

Jessie Chandler

RODERICK RALPH PETTY, THE Third, as opposed to the first, or even the second, regarded, through a blue-tinged haze of smoke, the homemade fruitcake that rested on his credenza. The muscles in his jaw bulged as he chewed thoughtfully on the end of an illegal Cuban stogie clenched between his yellowed teeth. The fruitcake was a Christmas gift someone had sent to his office. Roderick figured it was from one of his employees who didn't dare 'fess up.

Roderick was CEO of Petty Imports, a company he'd founded, and would likely die with since he didn't have any relatives who wanted anything to do with him or his business. Roderick had no close friends, and no blood family left alive. Employees and acquaintances trickled into his life, and strolled right back out when they realized that Petty wasn't just petty, but a tyrannical bastard to boot. He confided in no one, lunched with no one, golfed with no one.

His bride of all of eight months died in an unfortunate auto accident in the late Seventies, leaving him with a large life insurance settlement and her inheritance from her wealthy dead father's trust fund. Roderick never remarried, and company gossip claimed the old skinflint loved money more than he'd ever loved another living soul, his wife included. In-law gossip claimed that his wife's death wasn't an accident at all, just a way to get at her trust fund.

One thing that Roderick did enjoy, besides cold, hard cash, was fruitcake. It was the one redeeming thing to what he considered the worst holiday of all. Christmas. He detested the music, hated the garlands, and loathed the very spirit of the season.

In an attempt to keep up tradition, and at least for the sake of appearance, the employees who dared give him anything quickly figured out that the one present that wouldn't come hurling back at them was a gift of fruitcake.

A light tap on the solid mahogany office door pulled Roderick from his mouth-watering ruminations.

"What?" Roderick barked out of the side of his mouth that was unoccupied by the smoldering cigar.

After a moment of silence, Myra Andrews—Roderick's long suffering secretary— said, "I have one more. It's from me."

Roderick glared at the closed door for a moment. "Fine. Bring it in."

The door swung silently open, and Myra scuttled across the threshold, lips pursed in a perpetual lemon-face. Clad in tan, she looked like a skittish sparrow waiting for a cat to pounce on her. The only reason she was still with Roderick, and why a small core of loyal employees remained: Roderick Petty the Third paid his employees well to take the abuse he dished out.

"Put it there with the other one," he said with a nod of his head at the credenza. Myra knew better than to expect a thank you.

She set the cake down with an audible thud next to its mate. "Mr. Petty, it's after five. Would you mind—?"

"Oh, for Christ sake, go already." Roderick blew a stream of smoke at the gray-haired secretary, and rolled the stogie around his mouth. He then removed the cigar and licked his lips, annoyed that they felt like they were on fire and doubly so because he had no chapstick. Winter air in Minnesota tended to play hell with Roderick's lips, causing huge, unsightly cold sores. And he hated cold sores. They got in the way of the full enjoyment of his purloined cheroots.

"It's just that it's Christmas Eve—"

"Leave. I know what the day is, Ms. Andrews."

Myra Andrews backed out of the room, only turning away from Roderick as she pulled the door shut behind her.

. . . .

At exactly six pm, Roderick exited the elevator into the Petty Imports parking garage. Thankless employees, Roderick thought as he juggled the two gaily wrapped fruitcakes in one arm and attempted to retrieve the car keys from his black wool overcoat with his free hand. There was a time he'd stroll out of work with ten or more loaves. It usually depended on the economy. The worse it was, the more fruitcake he got.

The parking ramp was dim and mostly empty. Frigid gusts of wind blasted like mini-tornados past huge, exhaust-blackened concrete pillars, raising goosebumps on Roderick's arms. Cursing under his breath, he pressed the button on the key fob and the doors to his car unlocked with a muted click.

Roderick slid into the driver's seat, set the fruitcake next to him, and tugged the seatbelt around his rotund stomach. With a grunt, he slammed the door and started the battleship gray, late-model Mercedes. The engine roared to life and settled into a quiet purr as Roderick fired up another Havana and puffed the smoke into the dark interior of the car. As he inhaled, his throat began to burn. He took a sip from a half-frozen bottle of designer water he'd left in the beverage holder. All he needed was to come down with a cold. Or the Swine Flu.

With a disgusted sigh, Roderick exited the ramp and pointed the Mercedes in the direction of his in-law's place in St. Paul. Every Christmas Eve since Nadine had come to her unfortunate demise in a car accident back in '79, Roderick resentfully made the pilgrimage to the Dayton's Bluff estate.

In a strange, and to Roderick, completely ridiculous twist, in order to keep the trust fund he gained after Nadine died, he was compelled to appear at every Christmas gathering his wife's family held. Nadine's insufferable father, Harry Donaldson, wrote the clause into the will before a stroke gave him a slow, lopsided death. If Roderick missed so much as a single Christmas, the trust would revert to the family. The amount of money the trust provided each month coerced Roderick to comply, but not without plenty of rancor for the three remaining Donaldson siblings, their spouses, and their dreadful offspring.

As an added insult, the Donaldson family lawyer checked in each year to make sure Roderick followed Harry's wishes. So every December 24th, Roderick resignedly pointed his car toward his in-law's house and made his required appearance.

The drive between Petty Imports and the Donaldson's didn't take long. On the way, Roderick decided he'd give one of the fruitcakes to Nadine's family. Even if he didn't appreciate having to make his annual visit he never showed up empty-handed. He usually brought a bottle of Château La Vieille, but had not had time to pick up a bottle or send Myra out for one. The intent had been there, but Myra was on his back about this or that all day long, and now it was too late.

Gift decided, he made the appropriate turns on the twisted streets of St. Paul, and pulled to the curb in front of one of the oldest mansions in one of the oldest neighborhoods in the city. Even he grudgingly admitted the view there of the Mississippi River was breathtaking.

After a moment of consideration about which fruitcake to bring in, he took one last puff off his cigar, which irritated his throat even more. He hacked a moment, then stubbed the cigar out, tucked a loaf under his arm, and marched into his personal hell.

OPHELIA MOODY, NADINE'S SISTER, ushered Roderick into the beautifully decorated Donaldson house. Ophelia was a kind soul who did her best to steer clear of confrontation and strife. Roderick knew she was tired of his arrogance, frustrated by his condescension, and furious about the way he treated her two children, and those of her brother, Wyatt, and her sister, Joslyn. Therefore, he made a point of being as inhospitable as possible.

The mingled aromas of Christmas dinner floated from the kitchen throughout the house, and into the spacious entry. In spite of himself,

Roderick's mouth watered. Shrieks of delight from various grandkids filtered through the walls and grated on Roderick's brain.

"Here." He thrust the loaf of fruitcake at Ophelia as Joslyn, the oldest of the Donaldson siblings, waddled from the kitchen into the foyer, every year looking more like Andy Griffith's Aunt Bea.

"Why Roddy! It's so good of you to make it." Joslyn was the only one who dared called him Roddy.

He very obviously rolled his eyes and said, "We all know—"

"Oh, shush, you." Joslyn shooed Ophelia and a stone-faced Roderick into the cavernous living room. Wall sconces lent a gentle light to the room, which was dominated by a towering spruce, decorated to within an inch if its life. Glowing as if the tree had an unfortunate run-in with a high dose of radiation, Roderick wondered why the electrical circuits hadn't blown or why the house hadn't yet burned down. Every year the decorations grew increasingly overdone.

Two screeching kids stormed into the living room through one door and scooted out another, laughing hysterically. Roderick stepped out of the way and had to restrain himself from sticking a foot out and toppling one of the little monsters.

The scent of pine overwhelmed the smell of the cooking food. Roderick sniffed, enjoying the commingling of odors. He followed Ophelia to a side table next to the tree that held a crystal bowl filled with some kind of neon red-colored punch. Roderick knew from experience the punch packed a wallop.

Hors d'oeuvres sat on a tray beside the punch bowl. Ophelia unwrapped the fruitcake, sliced it, and went to work arranging it neatly on a platter. Roderick picked up a plate and loaded it with bite-sized-sandwiches, and ham and cream cheese-wrapped pickles. If he had to suffer through another Christmas Eve with these people, he wasn't going to leave hungry. Maybe this would be the year he'd really make a killing and be able to afford to lose Nadine's trust fund. However, the stock market was still in the doldrums, so that probably wasn't going to happen any time soon.

Ophelia straightened, dusted her hands, and disappeared down the hall without a word, presumably into the kitchen.

After taking four slices of fruitcake and placing them on top of the goodies on his plate, Roderick squared his shoulders and turned around to take in the picture-perfect living room scene.

Joslyn's husband, Malcolm, a coroner by trade, sat on a footstool, talking about the rising cost of pharmaceuticals with Wyatt, Nadine's brother, who was a pharmacist. Wyatt had been only fifteen when Nadine died, and he'd adored his older sister. After her death, Wyatt blamed Roderick for the accident. He was the one who kept the Roderick-Killed-Our-Sister story alive and well.

Carlos, Ophelia's husband, never said much to Roderick either, other than hello and goodbye, and an occasional "How 'bout them Vikes?" Seated by the picture window, the man was knee-deep into the punch, if the guffaws coming from him were any indication. Three of the grandchildren perched on the floor at his feet, listening intently to whatever tale he was weaving. Roderick heard Carlos mention seven-foot elves, outrageous gifts, and three-legged reindeer. After a disbelieving shake of his head, Roderick dove into the punch bowl for the first of what he was sure would be many cups of liquid tolerance.

Roderick took a sip of the syrupy concoction, wishing he'd brought his Château La Vieille after all. The uncultured taste buds of this family never changed. At least the drink soothed his throat, which was growing more sore by the moment. He settled into a chair in the corner of the room, where he could keep an eye on the goings-on, but stay off everyone's radar. Most of the clan ignored him anyway, and that suited him just fine.

Carefully, Roderick set the cup of punch on a coffee table next his chair, and balanced the plate of appetizers on his lap. He picked up a piece of the fruitcake, and opened his mouth to take a bite. A toddler bounced up to him, chubby little legs encased in red pants, his green, button-down shirt half-untucked. A smear of what looked like white frosting decorated the front of the boy's shirt.

The towhead, his mouth stained purple, balanced by putting his hand, sticky with God only knew what, on Roderick's knee. Roderick flinched, but held his ground for fear if he shifted, the kid would tumble onto him, and that was a horrifying thought. The kid wobbled as if he'd guzzled a gallon of the spiked punch.

Big, blue eyes peered up at him.

Fruitcake frozen near his mouth, Roderick squinted at the boy in displeasure. "What do you want, little brat?"

"You da money-gwubbah?" The boy had that hoarse, deep sound little kids' voices sometimes get.

"The what?" Roderick was pretty sure he knew which father the ankle-biter belonged to. Wyatt often lost his cool when he said much of anything to or about Roderick. The snot-faced urchin sounded just like him. Maybe if he throttled the kid, he could go home early.

"Asshoooole." The blue eyes never left Roderick's. The kid could have been a stunt double for the smarmy, disgusting twerp in that Meet the Parents movie.

"Gwubbah." The boy poked a finger in Roderick's belly and smacked his lips. "I'm tursty."

Roderick repressed the urge to take the kid by the ankles and dunk him in the punch bowl a few times. That should take care of the boy's need for fluids. Maybe if he offered him a bite of fruitcake, the rug-rat would shut up and go away. Roderick was just about to do that when Joslyn hustled into the living room, spotted the wayward child at Roderick's knee, and swooped over and gathered him up onto her hip.

"Sorry, Roddy, he's a sneak. I hope he didn't bother you too much." She gave Roderick a supercilious smile. "Dinner will be ready in about twenty minutes." Joslyn turned on her heel and headed out of the living room with her wayward charge. The boy watched Roderick over Joslyn's shoulder, pointed a bouncing finger at Roderick, and repeated, "Asshooooooole!"

Roderick clenched his teeth. What was this world coming to with youngsters like that? He downed the rest of his punch in one swallow.

He picked up the fruitcake again and took a healthy bite, chewing slowly, savoring the textures and spices. The cake had a subtle almond flavor he had not experienced before, and he thought the addition took the cake to another level altogether. There wasn't a note as to whom the gift was from, and although Roderick wouldn't have thanked the creator, he would not have hesitated to ask them to make him more.

Roderick ate all four slices, and was halfway through his plate of ham-wrapped pickles when the pain in his throat moved from smoldering to on-fire. His stomach began to heat up as well. He chewed the last pickle and swallowed, then sat stiffly, feeling very strange. The voices around him faded as his hands and feet started to twitch. The room grew larger, swelling and wavering, then shrank before his eyes. He heard himself saying something, but he couldn't understand what it was. Then Roderick stiffened, and tipped rather gracefully onto the thick pile carpet.

THE DAY BEFORE THE NEW YEAR dawned cold and clear. A small group of black-clad mourners lined up outside one of the mausoleums within the gated confines of Elm Haven Eternal Resting Grounds and Cemetery. The pastor entered the mausoleum, funeral urn in hand.

Joslyn and Malcolm, Ophelia and Carlos, Wyatt and Grace, and Myra Andrews crowded into the tight space and listened to the reverend attempt to talk about the non-existent redeeming qualities of the late Roderick Ralph Petty the Third. When the ashes to ashes and dust to dust finally settled, they all filed back out into the fresh, brisk air. After a short chat with the pastor, the mourners headed toward their respective cars. Wyatt hung back to allow Myra Andrews to catch up to him.

Her lemon-mouth frown had eased, and there was as close to a smile on her face as Wyatt had ever seen. He said, "Did you bring it?"

Myra's eyes glittered. "I did." She reached into her purse and pulled out a small brown paper bag. "Liquid nicotine. Who'd have thought just a few drops on the surface of his disgusting cigars would do the trick." She handed the bag to Wyatt. "The bottle you gave me is in there, and I got rid of the rest of the tainted cigars."

Wyatt nodded. "Liquid nicotine is incredibly toxic. Since the advent of smokeless cigarettes, liquid nic is sure a lot easier to get a hold of." Wisps of vapor floated around Wyatt's head as he spoke. "Malcolm has the doctor who signed the death certificate in his pocket, and he had the coroner's reports fixed so there aren't going to be any questions. Good old Roddy helped us out when he'd already chosen to be cremated."

"That was fortunate."

"As agreed, you'll stay on at Petty Imports, as CEO, which will soon be Donaldson Overseas."

Myra nodded, and one corner of her mouth lifted in a pleased half-smile. "I always told Mr. Petty smoking would kill him."

"Indeed. Happy New Year, Ms. Andrews."

"Yes, for once, Mr. Donaldson, it will be a very Happy New Year."

Jessie Chandler lives in Minneapolis, MN with her partner and two not-so-frisky felines. She is the author of the upcoming Midnight Ink release *The Bingo Barge Murder* (Spring 2011), and has a selection in the anthology *Women in Uniform: Medics and Soldiers and Cops, Oh My!* from Regal Crest Enterprises. Jessie is the Vice President of the Twin Cities chapter of Sisters in Crime, where she reviews a new mystery for the group every month. While Jessie isn't toiling away at the keyboard or reading her assigned novel of suspense and mayhem, she moonlights as the store manager for True Colors Bookstore (formerly Amazon Bookstore Cooperative), and sells unique, artsy T-shirts and other assorted trinkets to unsuspecting conference and festival goers in her spare time. You can check out her website at www.jessiechandler.com

Breakfast With Tiffany

Michael Allan Mallory

Honey, do you love me?"

"You bet," Jason answered through a spoonful of Cheerios, eyes on the sports page.

Tiffany shifted, leaving her toast untouched. "If I tell you something, you promise not to get mad?"

Jason flashed her an insincere smile. "Sure."

"I dented the minivan yesterday."

The spoon hovered near his mouth. Dumb bitch. Can't drive worth a damn. Can't do anything worth a damn. Still, a promise was a promise. Forcing himself to be cordial, he asked, "What did you do, back into a fire hydrant?"

"No, I ran over that woman you've been having sex with."

⁕ ⁕ ⁕

It was going to be a hell of a Christmas.

A surreal morning had morphed into a frantic afternoon, one which found Jason Craig wandering through the Westgate Outlet Mall with a growing sense of desperation. Still reeling from breakfast, he tried to make sense of Tiffany's story. At first he didn't believe her, given the muted nature of her emotions, not until she showed him the dent. The damage to the front bumper of their Dodge Caravan had sent a spike through his heart. What would that kind of impact do to human flesh? To Melissa?

He was desperate to know if it were all a spiteful joke. But Melissa hadn't answered her cell phone all day. Wasn't home. Wasn't at work.

He'd run out of options. They'd intentionally kept their affair low key, avoiding popular places and being seen. There was no one else to call.

Except the morgue.

Then, like a whisper in the wind, a snatch of conversation had drifted back from memory. Something about taking time off from her job to help her aunt at a kiosk at the Westgate Mall. True or not, it'd been enough to get him in his car on a snowy December afternoon and drive.

Once inside the mall he walked briskly across the mall's central courtyard, a man on a mission. Under the courtyard's vaulted glass roof, the outdoors had been brought inside in climate controlled comfort, a holiday winterscape of live spruce trees and mounds of artificial snow, colored lights and shiny ornaments. On the second level balcony, large pine bough wreaths hung with red ribbons. Festive holiday tunes played through the PA system to entertain shoppers. None of that mattered. All he cared about was finding the kiosk. Jason's last hope was to find Melissa there.

The escalator eased him down to the lower concourse as he gazed upon meandering throngs of shoppers in unzipped goosedown jackets or garish sweaters people only dared to wear at this time of year, improbable designs of candy red, kelly green and snow white. Human obstructions, that's all they were. Sucking in a breath, he zigzagged his way around them like an ambulance driver fighting through stalled traffic. By a chocolatier's stand he stopped in his tracks and wheeled around with the uncanny feeling he was being watched. Tinny seasonal tunes droned overhead as he searched nearby faces. Had Tiffany hired someone to keep tabs on him? Was that how she'd known about Melissa? Dismissing the thought, he put his legs in high gear. What did it matter now? Tiffany already knew about the affair.

He came across a cluster of free standing kiosks. One sold accessories for smart phones, while another vendor demonstrated his remote controlled miniature toy helicopters. After the fifth kiosk Jason began to wonder if he had come to the right mall. That's when he saw her. Eighty feet away at Icelandic Sheep Woollens, a slender dark-haired woman in a tight red sweater and form hugging black slacks. Her ready smile and fresh good looks were as inviting as a clear mountain lake. Melissa held some packages while an older, plumper, more conservatively dressed version of her adjusted a price tag by a stack of wool hats.

"Jason? What are you doing here?"

"You're—" He stopped. He couldn't blurt out she was supposed to be dead. Not in front of everyone.

"Jason? You look like you've seen a ghost."

"We need to talk."

"I go on break in fifteen minutes," Melissa told him, glancing at a Hispanic customer who examined a brown scarf.

He gestured toward the benches near a display of brown wicker reindeers draped in white mini-lights. "I'll be over there."

She nodded and turned to her customer who looked at her with amazement. "It's so soft! I've never felt wool so silky."

Jason Craig walked away on rubbery legs. Alive! Melissa was alive! It was all a bad dream—

He came to an abrupt stop.

If it wasn't Melissa Tiffany had run over, who was it? Or did it even happen? Maybe it was all a con job, a way to get him to lead them to Melissa as proof of his infidelity, whoever 'they' were. He wouldn't put it past Tiffany, though the plan did seem a little sophisticated for her.

But people change. No one stays the same. Not even him. He'd loved Tiffany once, with all the longing of love struck youth. In high school everything he did was in hopes of impressing her, to get her to notice him, to prove himself worthy. The prettiest girl in school, the sweetest and most popular, she was totally out of his league. From money. Not that it ever made any difference to her, she kept telling him. But it did to Jason, who'd always felt in the shadow of her parent's affluence.

He couldn't tell when things had changed between them, except that it started after her sickness began to define who she was, after medications changed her personality and made her space out half the time.

None of that mattered now. Melissa was alive! For the first time that day he felt relief and a sense the world would be right again. He smiled at a group of Victorian bell ringers as they rang out holiday tunes near the wicker reindeer.

"Jason."

He turned at the sound of Melissa's sweet voice. They embraced and kissed, he more passionately than her. "Jason?" she eyed him curiously after they parted. "What're you doing? You're the one who wanted to be careful in public."

"I don't care!" He laughed. "I'm thrilled to see you alive. And anyway, nobody's looking at us." He was right. Bag-burdened shoppers were either watching the bell ringers or were focused on finding their next purchase.

Melissa shot him a sidelong glance. "What's with you today? You're acting so . . . strange."

"I thought you were dead."

Her eyes narrowed. "Don't say that. It's not funny."

Jason pulled her away from the reindeer display, away from the crowd. He explained his breakfast conversation with Tiffany and all that had followed.

She gave him a hard look. "You saw the dent in the minivan? It's real?"

"Very real."

"Where is Tiffany?" Melissa glanced around anxiously. "She's not with you?"

"No. After breakfast she packed her bag and drove off to Thief River Falls to visit her sister. She's back tomorrow night, weather permitting. She just wanted to give me something to think about while she's gone."

"And she didn't sound angry?"

"The opposite. She was so blasé about everything, it was weird. Like she was in la-la land."

Melissa inhaled sharply. "It all makes sense now. My god . . ." Her eyes filled with a terrible understanding.

"Tiffany's off in her own little world," he tried to explain. "It's the meds. She's up to something. I just don't know what it is."

Melissa grabbed his arm. "Jason, how'd she find out about me?"

"She didn't say and I didn't ask. It was bad enough I thought you were dead. She must be nuts to make up a story like that, Mel."

"It's not a story, Jason. Linda's dead. My next door neighbor? You met her once. Two days ago she was run over by a hit and run driver in front of my house."

"Your house?"

Melissa shuddered as she recalled something else. "Linda even looks a bit like me. She was at my place to give my cat his insulin shot because I was here. Tiffany must've been waiting outside. Don't you get it? Tiffany thought Linda was me!"

"It wasn't a made up story? Tiffany really did it, ran over someone?"

"We have to call the police. Turn her in."

He felt the heat of Melissa's indignation, even admired it, that fire in her soul was what made her exciting. "Yes," he agreed, racing through the possibilities: Tiffany is arrested. Goes to trial. With his testimony and the evidence of the minivan she's convicted of murder. Then jail. Incredible, he thought, she'd be out of the way by her own actions. It was perfect. Except for one thing—

"Jason. What is it?"

"Maybe we ought to think this through before we get the police involved."

"Think it through? The woman killed my neighbor. Almost killed me! We're not letting her get away with this."

"Keep it down." His eyes flicked toward passing shoppers, none of whom showed interest in them. "Tiffany might not do any jail time. Given her recent behavior and the pills, a good lawyer could convince a jury she wasn't in her right mind. She could get off."

Melissa shook her head in disbelief.

Jason took her hand, savoring its softness. "What about our plans? For months we've talked about running off to Seattle next summer. I've been squirreling away cash. We'll need it all to start a new life together. The catch is I work for Tiffany's father. If she's arrested for killing Linda, she'll say it was you she was really trying to run down. Then she'll explain why she wanted you dead. Roger will fire my sorry ass immediately, believe me. That'll cut off the cash flow sooner than expected."

"So we're letting her off the hook?"

"Of course not. But there may be other options."

"Like what?"

He hesitated, aware he was heading into dangerous waters.

Melissa's gaze locked onto him. "What other options?"

His tongue swiped across dry lips. Jason was at the edge of the precipice; it was now or never.

"We kill her," he said.

Melissa stared back in disbelief. "We can't do that. It's—it's wrong."

"I know, darling. But wasn't it wrong of her to mercilessly run down your neighbor? That was supposed to be you."

She wrapped her arms around herself. "I could never kill another person."

He took her by the shoulders. "And you won't have to. I'll handle everything."

She shook her head. "It's still wrong." This time with less conviction.

"We had a plan, darling. Tiffany nearly ruined it. She could still ruin it...unless we stop her."

"I don't know . . ."

"We can make this work," he came back. "Just hear me out. When Tiffany gets back tomorrow, I'll be the contrite husband. Tell her I've been a fool. I'll say I've broken it off with you and come to realize how important she is to me. She'll lap it up."

Circling his arm round Melissa's waist, he guided her away from prying ears. He spoke cautiously. "We've got ticket's to the Guthrie's *A Christmas Carol*. Tiffany loves that show. Afterwards, we'll drive around neighborhoods and look at holiday lights." Jason's eyes did a quick scan to make sure no one was listening in. "We'll detour to a parking lot in a rough neighborhood, it's a big park and ride lot. That's where I'll do it. I'll get her out of the car on some pretense and knock her head against the fender. I'll say we were jumped by a gang of punks. I fought back but there were too many of them."

"That won't work. It sounds phony."

"That's where you come in."

"Me? Oh no, I told you—"

"Don't worry. You won't have to go near Tiffany. Like I said, I'll handle that. What you do is show up afterwards. I need to look like I got beat up too. You gotta smack me a few times with a baseball bat, use the bottom of your shoe on my face so I have abrasions and bruises, things I couldn't have done to myself."

"Hit you? I—couldn't."

"Yes you can, darling. Maybe when you see Tiffany on the ground you'll think of poor Linda in the street."

"I suppose," Melissa murmured, not quite convinced.

"Don't go overboard with the baseball bat," he added with a nervous laugh. "Just a few smacks, enough to convince the cops it was a real attack. You don't have to break any bones."

She thought it over. "Will it work?"

"Sure it will. I'll call 911 and do my act for the cops. You'll be long gone before they show up."

Melissa glanced over her shoulder. "I've got to get back."

He moved in to close the deal. "Darling, we can do this. It's the best way. If Tiffany dies from a random act of street violence, we're home free. I get everything. The house. The bank account. The Seattle move'll be a breeze. You gotta tell me you're in."

For a moment she teetered on the edge of indecision. "Okay, I'm in." Her voice was tight. "But how'll I find your car? Where's this parking lot?"

From his pocket he pulled out a scrap of paper on which he scrawled directions. "You know my car. Here's the license plate number and the location of the lot. Figure about 11:30 on Thursday evening."

"Okay." She fidgeted. "My aunt's waiting."

"Just tell me you'll be there."

A deep breath. "I'll be there. I may hate myself later but I'll be there."

"You've got to be. It all hinges on you. I'll get the bat to you this evening. If we do this thing right we'll be home free."

WHAT A FUN SHOW, JASON. THANK YOU." Tiffany smiled broadly as they exited the theater. Around them people buttoned up coats against the cold bite of evening. "Such a great story. And so uplifting."

"It is," he agreed and meant it. The Guthrie's adaptation of *A Christmas Carol* was an old favorite. In the early days of their courtship he and Tiffany came to the show every year; in fact, decades ago it was a pair of free tickets that had motivated a socially awkward Jason Craig to dredge up the courage to ask out the prettiest girl at Central High.

In the near distance the downtown skyline shined in the dark like a giant holiday display. A light snow dusted them. Tiffany, mindful of the slush, stepped off the curb with a grunt.

"Your hip bothering you again?"

"A little. It's not so bad." She smiled, clutching a tiny polar bear plush toy close. He'd surprised her with the gift, which she held on to as if it were the most precious thing in the world. It didn't take much to make her happy, he thought.

They were among a river of theater patrons making for the parking ramp across the street. A cold gust whipped the snow around them. Tiffany snuggled into her coat collar. "The play was just terrific." Her sweet face looked at him meaningfully. "And you've been so fun to be around, Jason. Like when we first dated. These last few days have been wonderful."

"You deserve it. I behaved like an ass. Took you for granted. That won't ever happen again. I promise."

She sighed. "It's been so long since I've heard you talk to me that way. I've missed it."

The serenity of her smile and the affection behind it touched him. He'd forgotten how radiant Tiffany could be when she was happy; maybe because he hadn't given her much cause to be happy in recent few years.

"I spoke to Daddy yesterday."

Jason slowed, tensing up. "Oh, about what?"

"About you," she answered coyly.

If she'd told the old man about Melissa, he was sunk!

"About me?" he probed further, trying to mask his concern. "Something good, I hope."

"It was. I told Daddy how wonderful you've been."

"Anything else . . . sweetheart?"

"I don't think so."

"You didn't mention the little discussions we've had recently?"

"Gracious, no!" She pooh-poohed. "That's between you and me. I'd never tell him that. You know how he gets. Oh"—her face brightened—"he said something about a promotion for you soon. Isn't it wonderful?"

Wonderful. And unexpected. Jason smiled, charmed by Tiffany's buoyant outlook and the ease with which she'd handled her father, a man who didn't easily let go of grudges. She didn't have to do that; she could have made Jason's life miserable. Her thoughtfulness gave him pause to reflect. The sweet face gazing back at him transported Jason to another lifetime when he was a gawky teen and she was the eighteen-year-old beauty who'd stolen his heart. A swirl of emotions told him he still cared about her. And if that were true how could he carry out his plan? Could he really kill the woman who'd meant the world to him at one time? The answer, he realized with a heavy heart, was no.

He couldn't do it.

The realization hit him like a January wind chill. Jason knew everything had changed now. He had to let Melissa know. She'd be waiting.

"Jason?" Tiffany looked back with concern. "Is something wrong?"

"The parking ramp," he said, covering the slip. "It's packed. Everyone's gonna try to get out at once." Just beyond the ramp, a block away, a bright neon marquee caught his eye. "Maxines. Hey, we haven't been there in ages. How about a drink? We'd just be stuck behind a line of cars for thirty minutes."

"Maybe something hot." Tiffany buried herself deeper into her coat collar. The snow was coming down harder.

They stepped onto Washington Avenue and hurried to avoid oncoming traffic. As they reached the opposite curb, Tiffany's heel slipped on the slush.

"Careful." Jason steadied her. "It's getting icy."

Tiffany's silver blue eyes glistened in the lamplight. "Remember the time we went ice skating with Gary and he kept falling down?"

"Your cousin Gary?"

"Yeah, on Lake Minnetonka."

"That was back in high school! Gary'd never been on skate's before. He talked like he knew what he was doing, but he kept falling on his ass."

"He got madder and madder."

"Man, he was furious." Jason laughed.

Maxine's was coming up fast. He glanced at the old brick façade, flanked on either side by juniper bushes wrapped in spirals of cranberry-colored mini lights. Jason and Tiffany converged with another group headed toward the restaurant.

With relish, Jason remembered how the story ended. "Gary got so pissed he finally yelled at his feet, 'I've had enough of you dumb ass skates!'"

An older woman with a pinched face and blaze orange hair scowled at Jason as he brushed by her on the sidewalk leading to Maxine's. Jason and Tiffany climbed the eight concrete steps up to the vintage double doors when he felt a sudden movement. Tiffany's foot had slipped on a piece of ice. A horrified gasp escaped her as she fell back, arms flailing helplessly toward him. Instinctively, he reached out. His fingers brushed her arm, catching on something for an instant before her weight and inertia ripped her from his grasp. Stunned, he watched her tumble backward and down. She landed hard on the cement steps, cracking her head.

Jason watched in stunned silence.

Gasps and cries nudged him into awareness. A young woman in a light parka and Peruvian stocking hat rushed to Tiffany's side. Only then did he realize something was in his hand. His gaze dropped to his still clenched fingers to see the head of the little plush polar bear.

"Call 911!" someone cried.

"It's too late." The young woman displayed her bloodied palm. "I'm an RN. She's dead."

Dead?

He blinked, just now comprehending. Tiffany was dead from her own clumsiness. An accident. In front of witnesses. It couldn't have worked out better if he'd planned it. And yet, in spite of this amazing piece of luck, he felt no pleasure at her death, only sadness. Even shame.

"Sir," the young woman asked, "are you all right?"

"What a horrible accident," was all he could manage. The surprising thing to him was he meant it.

"Wait! Wait!" A voice protested from below. The orange-haired woman hurried up the steps, her bony fingers gripping the wrought iron hand rail for support. "Call the police. This was no accident. He pushed her. I saw it!"

Jason's mouth fell open.

"He pushed her." The woman insisted to the others who had gathered around the stairs.

"I didn't push her. She slipped."

"You pushed her. You were arguing with her a second ago."

"Arguing? We weren't arguing."

"Don't lie to me. I heard. You called her a...dumb ass," the old woman added with distaste, as though she could barely force herself to say the words.

Two middle-aged women on the step near Jason gave him the evil eye.

"That wasn't what it was," Jason explained. "It was a funny story—"

"You call this funny, young man?" The woman with the fiery hair pointed to Tiffany. "I know what I heard and what I saw. You pushed her! You saw it, didn't you?" she challenged a young mother two steps down.

The seed was planted. "Well—Yes, I did. His arm flew out. He must've pushed her."

"I saw it too," volunteered a bearded man on the sidewalk.

Jason clapped his hands on top of his head. "I didn't push her!"

The old woman was resolute. "You killed her. We all saw it and that's what we'll tell the police. You won't get away with this."

Every face around him looked back with suspicion. Jason's shoulders sagged under the weight of their accusation, as cold reality told him his fate was already sealed. In silent acquiescence, his fingers relaxed and let the head of the plush toy fall, where it bounced silently down the steps and into oblivion.

Michael Allan Mallory is the co-author of *Death Roll*. His debut novel with Marilyn Victor was published in hardcover in 2007 and featured mystery's first zoologist sleuth: zookeeper Lavender "Snake" Jones. Several of Michael's short stories have made it into print, most notably his appearance in the *Resort to Murder* anthology published by the Minnesota Crime Wave. *Killer Instinct*, the second Snake Jones novel, will be published in December 2010. Set in Ely, Minnesota, *Killer Instinct* pits Snake against a resolute double murderer as she explores the fascinating world of the gray wolf. Though he wishes he could write full-time, Michael currently spends his daytime hours working with computers in the Information Technology field. He lives in St. Louis Park with his delightful wife and two large and bodacious cats. His website is www.snake-jones.com

The Blackest Friday

Brian Landon

AFTER FRANTICALLY SEARCHING the crowded, bustling main floor of the Mall of America on the busiest shopping day of the year, Officer Glenn Hanratty discovered his nephew Aaron was high on SpongeBob.

The ten-year-old waved to him from atop the cartoon-themed roller coaster as it made its decent down a steep decline, followed by several loops and spirals. Hanratty was feeling nauseous just watching it, a combination of motion sickness-by-proxy and panic-fueled adrenaline. Although, he felt relieved that Aaron was safe on a roller coaster rather than abducted by some amusement park-dwelling pervert. He heard those stories all too much in his line of work.

Not that Officer Hanratty did much investigating. He wasn't that kind of officer. At least, not anymore. He'd been a Lieutenant in the late nineties until his eensie-weensie drinking problem surfaced and never went away. Now he took crime scene photos. He also got to ride the MPD's only Schwinn. He tried to not brag about such things too often.

"Do you want to sit on Santa's lap?" asked Hanratty.

Aaron rolled his eyes. "Do I look like I'm five?"

"No," said Hanratty. "But you look like a kid who'd rather not have a lump of coal in his stocking. And you know what Santa hates more than anything? Sarcasm."

Aaron scrunched his eyes, deep in thought. "Well, I guess I do want a new bike."

"Same here. Let's go see Santa."

Hanratty kept his hand on Aaron's shoulder as they plowed their way through a thick crowd of mall shoppers, all of whom were loaded up with bags, coats, and gaggles of small children in strollers.

"Where is Santa?" asked Aaron.

"Just ahead, near Nordstrom's," said Hanratty. "And if the line is too long, there's another one over by Sears."

Aaron looked puzzled. "How can there be two Santas?"

"Not two," said Hanratty. "Four. One in each corner of the mall. That way, people don't have to wait for hours, and they can continue shopping and spending their hard-earned money on over-sized sunglasses and plastic shoes with holes in them."

"But how can Santa be in four places at once?"

"Do you really think the Santa Claus has time to hang around malls right before Christmas? During the busiest toy-making season? No, no, no. Santa hires these guys to fill in for him."

Aaron seemed to consider the logic. "Then how does the real Santa know what I want for Christmas?"

"The Santas who work here will relay the info back to the real Santa, so he knows," said Hanratty.

"Then why don't I just send a letter directly to Santa? Or e-mail him?"

"You can e-mail Santa?" asked Hanratty. It was his turn to be confused.

"Yup. He's on Facebook, too."

"Huh," said Hanratty.

As they neared what looked like an immobile parade float caked in fake snow, it became clear that this must be one of the more popular Kris Kringles.

"Let's go find the Sears' Santa," said Hanratty. "The Nordstrom's Santa has fifty kids waiting in line."

Hanratty turned away with his hand still on Aaron's shoulder when he felt a tug on his jacket. He also noticed that the volume of the crowd increased three fold.

"Uncle Glenn?"

Hanratty could barely hear his nephew. What was the deal with middle-aged soccer moms screaming all the time?

"Why is Santa playing paintball?"

Hanratty looked where Aaron was pointing. He found it odd that they were able to replace the white confetti with red confetti so quickly. Why red snow?

Then he noticed Santa slouching in his chair, a spray of blood spurting out of his neck and landing on the stage.

"That wasn't a paintball," said Hanratty, covering Aaron's eyes with his hand.

Hanratty carefully scanned the milling spectators on all three floors. It was impossible to see anything suspicious in a sea of so many people.

He pulled out his cell phone and called 911. Dozens of shoppers already had their phones out, but Hanratty wouldn't feel right about assuming they were calling the police. For all he knew, they could be recording video for YouTube.

"Can I look yet?" asked Aaron.

"No," said Hanratty. He heard a voice coming from his cell. "Yes, I'm at the Mall of America –"

"Is this the Santa incident? We already know," said the voice. "Let me take down your name and number, and an officer will follow up with you."

"No need," said Hanratty. "This is Officer Glenn Hanratty. I'm on scene. Off-duty. I'll call back in if I get any further information."

He hung up, then put his cell phone back into his pants pocket, then reached into his coat and took out a small, digital camera.

"You know, you could probably take photos with your phone. Cameras are kind of pointless."

"No, they're not. Hey – why are you looking?"

Aaron shrugged. "I'll be a cop someday. I might as well get used to this."

Hanratty was doing what he does best, other than drinking. He snapped photos of everything. The stage. The crowd behind them. Dead Santa.

"You're going to be a cop?" said Hanratty. "Alright. Who do you think did this?"

"The Easter Bunny?" asked Aaron.

"Is that a joke?" asked Hanratty.

"Yeah, sorry," said Aaron. "Just trying to lighten the mood."

As Hanratty took photos, he saw tons of weeping children, as well as the horrified looks on their parents' faces.

"I see what you mean," said Hanratty. "Don't worry. Cops crack jokes all the time. It's called a defense mechanism."

Aaron nodded. "But seriously, the killer is on the second floor."

"What?"

Hanratty spun around and took several snapshots of the people standing behind the second floor railing.

"Where?" asked Hanratty.

"Oh, he's not there now. At least, I don't think so. But the bullet definitely came from there."

Hanratty stopped taking photos and studied his nephew.

"How do you know this? Did you see him?"

Aaron shook his head. "No, but check this out." He grabbed Hanratty's hand and yanked. Hanratty was a bit startled by his nephew's enthusiasm.

"Where are we going?"

"Over here," said Aaron. He pulled Hanratty around the stage and towards one of the storefronts.

"Why are we going to the Baby Gap?"

"Just c'mon," he said. "Look." He pointed to a small, perfectly circular hole towards the bottom of the plexi-glass window.

"Huh," said Hanratty. "I'll be damned." He took photos of the bullet hole.

"I figure, if the killer was on our level, the bullet would have to go upward, right? But if this bullet hole is down here, that means the killer was on the second or third floor. And if you look up where the third floor is, there's no way the bullet would reach this window. It would have gone directly into the floor."

"You're embarrassingly good at this," said Hanratty.

Aaron grinned. "Thanks."

Holding tightly onto Aaron's hand, Hanratty pushed through the torrent of shoppers. One particularly rotund woman nearly shoved Hanratty head-first into the Piercing Pagoda, but Aaron managed to steady his uncle before any damage was done. Then, with the exception of a few stragglers, the crowd had all but disappeared. Hanratty assumed most had left the mall completely, although many may have ran to the opposite side of the mall, hoping they were safe from danger. Hanratty didn't think anyone was safe yet.

Hanratty and Aaron ran down the nearly vacant hallway until they reached a familiar scene. Blood spattered over fake snow. Another Santa slumped over in his chair. This Santa, however, had lifeless eyes that stared directly where Hanratty was standing. Aaron must have felt the eyes on him too, because he let out a whimper.

"It's okay," said Hanratty. "This is a good sign. He was probably staring in this direction because he caught sight of the killer. We're probably standing right where the shooter was."

A small army of police officers burst in through the mall entrance. Hanratty recognized a few them, including Officer McNulty, whom he often found himself on the wrong side of an argument with. Hanratty knew McNulty and his team would follow standard emergency protocol, but he didn't trust that they'd listen to his theory about where the shooter was going next. Hanratty, due to his drinking problem and a few other embarrassing incidents, didn't garner the most respect from his peers.

"We should run," said Hanratty.

"Why?" asked Aaron.

"Because if my theory is correct, the Santa killer is following a counter-clockwise pattern, and is heading for the Macy's Santa next. If we can get there fast enough, we can at least catch him in the act and possibly . . ." Hanratty cringed, "stop him."

"How are we going to stop him?" asked Aaron.

"I haven't thought that far ahead yet. Let's make a run for it."

Running through the mall had become substantially easier now that most of the shoppers had seemingly become aware that something horrible was happening, and thus evacuated the mall. Unfortunately, it also meant that McNulty could see exactly where he was headed, and decided to give chase himself. To Hanratty's dismay, it seemed McNulty didn't trust Hanratty in the least. He probably suspected Hanratty of going on an excessively drunken shoot-em-up bender, killing a bunch of Santas in the process.

"Let's go up to the second floor," said Hanratty, panting. He wasn't used to this much exercise, except for the occasional bicycle-ride when he needed to get around town.

"Why?" asked Aaron.

"Because, I doubt we can stop this guy from the bottom floor if he's up there," said Hanratty.

"Okay," said Aaron, sounding apprehensive and out of breath. "You're the professional."

That made Hanratty feel apprehensive. At least McNulty was a good ways behind them.

Hanratty and his nephew ran up the escalator and continued down the second floor hallway towards Macy's.

Suddenly, Hanratty was stopped dead in his tracks when a hand grabbed his jacket.

"Excuse me, sir," said a voice. "Have you ever had a manicure?"

Hanratty turned and glared and the young, blonde woman who stood in front of a Miracle Nail kiosk. She had a crazy Stepford Wife gaze.

"Can't you see I'm running?" asked Hanratty.

"Yes, and the sweat is going to dry out your skin something terrible. We have a tremendous line of lotions available."

"Get your hand off me," said Hanratty. He could see McNulty was fast approaching.

"Not until you moisturize," said the woman, squirting a dollop of white cream on Hanratty's hand.

Hanratty wiped the cream on the sleeve of the woman's pink linen blouse, grabbed the bottle of lotion, and threw it over the railing, onto the first floor.

"I don't want your damn lotion," said Hanratty. "Listen a little more closely next time."

The woman shook her head. "Big mistake," she said.

Hanratty sneered at her, took Aaron's hand, and continued to run. Within seconds, a high school kid in a business suit was running alongside Hanratty with a clipboard in his hands.

"Are you interested in taking a survey regarding your mall experience?" said the kid.

Hanratty grabbed the clipboard and threw it behind an Orange Julius counter.

"A verbal response would have sufficed," the kid said.

"Go fuck yourself," said Hanratty.

The kid stopped running alongside Hanratty and instead stood in place with a disappointed look on his face.

They kept running, but Aaron turned to look behind him.

"That was kind of mean," said Aaron.

"I'm sorry," said Hanratty. "But I've always wanted to do that."

"We can stop running now," said Aaron. "We're at Macy's." Hanratty put on the brakes. He held onto the railing to catch his breath, peered over, and was happy to see that this Santa was very much alive. Santa and his elf friends looked around with dumbfounded expressions. Clearly, no one had passed the word that a Santa killer was on the loose.

Just as a sweaty, angry Officer McNulty grabbed Hanratty by the collar and was likely about to say something unpleasant, screams erupted from the other side of the mall.

"Shit," said Hanratty.

"You know what's happening here, don't you?" asked McNulty.

"Obviously, someone is going around the entire mall, killing each of the four Santas," said Hanratty.

"Not this one, though?" asked McNulty.

"Whoever is doing this killed the Nordstrom's Santa first, then the Sears' Santa. We assumed he was going in a counter-clockwise pattern, but after shooting the second Santa, he must have cut through the amusement park in the middle of the mall."

"So he just killed the Bloomingdale's Santa," said Aaron. "Which only leaves Macy's. The last one."

"You should really get this kid out of here," said McNulty.

Aaron shook his head. "I'm going to be a cop."

"Whatever, kid. Just don't get yourself killed, okay?"

"I'll try."

Hanratty put his hand on his nephew's shoulder.

"Here's what we're going to do," said McNulty. "If the Santa killer is coming this way, let's all get behind that baseball hat kiosk and wait for him."

"What'll you do then?" asked Hanratty.

McNulty took his gun out of its holster. "I'll take him out."

"He's not going to be on this floor," said Aaron.

"What?" asked McNulty. "What the hell are you talking about?"

"He had to go down to the first floor in order to cut through the middle of the mall. There's no way to do that on the second floor . . . it's just one big circle."

McNulty glared at Hanratty's nephew. "He could come back up an escalator."

"He could, but I doubt it," said Aaron. "But hey, it's your call. You seem to know what you're doing."

McNulty frowned. "Okay, so what would you do, you little sarcastic pri—"

Hanratty held up a hand, silencing McNulty.

"We should go down there and get Santa far away. If the killer can't find Santa, then he won't be able to do anything."

"That's *one* way of doing it," said McNulty, grumbling.

"We better hurry," said Hanratty. He grabbed Aaron's hand and they ran down the Macy's escalator.

Santa appeared delighted to finally have a customer.

"Ho ho ho, young man! What would you like for Christmas?"

Hanratty grabbed Santa by his red felt coat. "You're coming with us."

Santa's elf friends scampered away. Santa looked stunned and a bit frightened. He looked questioningly at Aaron. "It's for your own good," said Aaron.

Santa didn't seem to find this very reassuring.

"Help!" yelled Santa.

McNulty, who was standing behind Aaron and Hanratty, pointed his gun at Santa.

"We're the police," said McNulty.

Santa looked at Aaron again.

"Not him," said McNulty. "But the two of us. Just come with us right now. Someone has already killed the other three Santas."

Santa's jaw dropped.

Hanratty whispered into Aaron's ear. Aaron nodded. Aaron took Santa by the hand and said, "Come with me."

Hanratty watched as Aaron took Santa into a nearby Old Navy. He felt they'd be somewhat safe hiding out in the dressing rooms.

McNulty and Hanratty stood behind a decorative plastic fern. McNulty was at the ready, like a hound that caught scent of a squirrel.

A few minutes passed. Hanratty was beginning to suspect that whoever was so angry at Santa Claus that he wanted to kill them all may have abandoned his operation and left the mall altogether.

But wouldn't you know it, his little nephew was right. Stumbling along the hallway – on the first floor, just like he predicted – was a man that looked more than a little suspicious. He wore a suit that was probably red at some point, but was currently a grimy brown. He had a full, bushy brown beard. His rosy cheeks matched his rosy bloodshot eyes. A damp stain in the front of his trousers was spreading as he walked. He held a gun in one hand and a half-eaten candy cane in the other.

"Holy shit," whispered McNulty. He stood up from behind the fern. "Stop! Police! Drop your gun!" he yelled, pointing his gun directly at the bad Santa.

Hanratty was snapping photos. Of the shooter. McNulty. Everything.

The bad Santa was whipping his arm around towards McNulty when a scream ripped through the mall.

"Don't shoot him!" yelled the voice. The bad Santa dropped his gun when he recognized who it was. The blonde woman from the Miracle Nail kiosk.

"I did it honey," said the bad Santa, hiccupping. "Juss like you said."

Within seconds, McNulty was putting handcuffs on the Santa. He didn't seem too interested in explanations.

Hanratty, however, was interested. And he knew who would be even more interested. Aaron.

He fetched the Macy's Santa and Aaron from the Old Navy dressing room.

"You have him? He's arrested?" asked the Macy's Santa.

"We do," said Hanratty. "Right out here. Let me know if you recognize him."

As soon as they reached the Old Navy exit and caught a view of what could have been a nasty crime scene, Macy's Santa said, "Oh, boy."

"You know him?" asked Hanratty.

"Herbert Lanford," said Macy's Santa. "He was the fifth Santa."

"You mean, he was hired here?" asked Hanratty.

"Not exactly," said Macy's Santa. "He didn't quite make the cut. They probably would have hired him if it weren't for his background check."

"Not good?" asked Hanratty.

Macy's Santa nodded, and looked down at Aaron. "He was a real naughty boy this year." Aaron and Macy's Santa both laughed, as if they were both enjoying their own inside joke.

As they got closer, Hanratty couldn't help listen to the lovers spat between the kiosk woman and the deranged Santa killer.

"I never told you to do this," insisted the blonde woman. She looked nervously at McNulty. "Why would you say that, Herbert?"

"You tole me I had ta get a job at any cost so we can keep our apartments. So I did – I got rid of the other Santa Clauseses, so they have to hire *me* now." He hiccupped again.

"You're going to be in prison," said the kiosk lady.

"Judge'll understan' " said Herbert Lanford.

The kiosk woman got closer to Lanford. She plugged her nose while she looked at his dirty, ragged appearance. Taking a step behind him, next to McNulty, she looked at his hands.

"Your cuticles are . . ." she was fighting back nausea, "filthy. We're done, Herbert. I never want to see or hear from you ever again."

"What I do?" he asked, as backup officers arrived, helping McNulty lead Herbert Lanford, the Fifth Santa, towards the exit and the back of a warm, comfortable police car on the way to a cold, unforgiving jail cell.

T HAT'S REALLY TOO MUCH," said Hanratty.

"Not at all," said Macy's Santa. "One bike for each of you is the least I owe you for saving my life."

"But really, you don't–"

"No, no," said Santa. "I've made my list and checked it twice. There's no doubt about it. I owe you and young Aaron one bicycle a piece. The list never lies."

Hanratty shrugged. "Fair enough," he said. He shook Santa's hand. Santa rubbed the top of Aaron's head, which Aaron didn't much care for, but let it slide anyway.

WELL," SAID Hanratty, as he and Aaron walked out the door into the chilly Minnesota night. "I've never lied about the fact that I have a drinking problem. However, I can honestly say it's never been *that* bad."

"I would hope not," said Aaron.

Hanratty kneeled down and looked Aaron directly in the eyes. "You know, when you were hiding in Old Navy, you really didn't need to tell him we wanted bikes for Christmas."

"I didn't," said Aaron.

Hanratty paused. "What?"

"I didn't say we wanted anything."

Hanratty looked inquiringly at his young nephew, but saw no signs of a fib. Hanratty looked back at the mall behind them. Then back at his nephew.

"Let's swing by the bar on the way home."

Brian Landon lives in Blaine, MN, and is the author of the Doyle Malloy mystery series. His debut novel, *A Grand Ol' Murder*, was nominated for the Minnesota Book Award and the Midwest Book Award. The second and most recent volume, *The Case of the Unnecessary Sequel*, was released in the Spring of 2010. Set in Brainerd, *The Case of the Unnecessary Sequel* involves an investigation following the murder of an actor on the set of *Fargo II: Midwest Bugaloo*. Visit Brian at www.brianlandon.com

Sweet as Pie

Camille Hyytinen

As human beings, we all have but one desire—to be happy. But at what price is happiness obtained?

The pain of divorce was almost worse than death, after being married twenty-five years. Six months into her newfound freedom, Vanessa Chandler spent most of her time divided between three things—work, her sixteen-year-old son, CJ, and most recently, her neighbor, Mildred Nelson, or Millie as she was known in most circles. Millie had been there for Vanessa; through tears and anger, and all the injustices life threw in her face daily since the bitter divorce. The old woman was therapeutic. Good advice along with a grandmotherly presence kept Vanessa coming back. It helped that CJ liked her, too. She always had freshly baked cookies waiting and paid him handsomely for shoveling her walkway in winter or mowing the lawn in summer.

Vanessa grabbed her purse, thinking about Millie's excitement when they spoke on the phone. Her friend had urged her to hurry before the storm hit. The weatherman was saying four inches by noon, and an additional four to eight inches of snow by early evening.

She left the house, wondering how many pies she'd be carrying when she returned several hours later. CJ would be happy. Apple pie was one of his favorites. She smiled thinking of her son. They had been through a lot lately, but had developed a stronger mother-son relationship because of it. Once Bill left, and the constant tension and fighting were eliminated, time spent together was actually pleasant. They had the same sense of humor and found that sometimes laughter could get them through the most difficult days. *Everything happens for a reason*, her mother used to say.

She still thought of Alan frequently, the other man who had turned her world—and everyone else's—upside down, and then *poof* was gone. He was now happily married. Vanessa couldn't fathom the thought of even starting another relationship. *Get burned and learn* was her mantra lately. Plus, twenty-five years with William J. Chandler was enough to last a lifetime. The first half of their marriage was relatively good. It was after CJ was born, they'd discovered issues. Bill never wanted children and deeply resented any time she spent tending to their son. As CJ grew older, Bill tried to bond with the boy, but his half-hearted attempts were too little, too late. They all drifted further and further apart until finding their way back was virtually impossible, especially after the infidelity.

Things had changed now. *Change is good,* she kept telling herself. Vanessa was content to live alone with her teenage son, go to work, visit Millie, and repeat the process—nothing more. There was no need to find another mate . . . at least not yet, maybe never.

THIS WAS THE MOST IMPORTANT TIME of year in Millie's mind. The eighty-seven-year-old woman had survived two husbands, birthed five children who procreated twelve grandchildren, and made the best apple pie in the entire world. With the annual Christmas bake-off contest only two days away, time was running out to ensure the prize-winning pie was prepared for display at the Apple Valley Senior Community Center. The bake-off started the winter carnival festivities put on by the Lutheran church next door, along with other local business affiliates—every year for the past decade. The contest, followed by a Christmas dinner at the church in the evening, was a crowd-pleaser and initiated five days of pure carnival fun. The carnival was small in comparison to the one held in St. Paul annually, but helped raise much needed funds for the homeless shelter. It was held on church grounds which bordered the community center and offered everything from face-painting to snow sculptures, mini donuts to snow-cones.

Millie had won a blue ribbon every year since it began, except last year. Last year it went to a new up-and-comer, Henry Baker, who lived two and half blocks away in their quiet little neighborhood in Apple Valley, Minnesota. Johnny Cake Ridge Road hadn't been the same since the Bakers moved in eighteen months ago. Rumor had it the Bakers were swingers. Henry Baker's wife was twenty years younger and very beautiful, which didn't help to squelch wagging tongues.

As was standard procedure, Mildred practiced the art of pie baking days before she delivered the final product. It was all in the flaky crust and the right apples of course. She had always used Granny Smith apples. Henry Baker used something else . . . She knew he had them flown in special from somewhere, but he'd never divulged exactly where.

Ingredients lined the counter—shortening, flour, cinnamon and secret spices, sugar, a variety of apples—along with a wooden rolling pin and four pie pans. Millie picked up a Honey Crisp—the Minnesota apple—and held it to her nose, inhaling deeply. "Perhaps this is the secret."

The doorbell rang and the old woman almost skipped to the door, flinging it open. "Vanessa! You made it in record time. Is CJ still sleeping?"

Vanessa grinned. "What do you think? It's Christmas vacation and he's sixteen."

"I think . . . " Millie's blue eyes twinkled mischievously. "I wish I was sixteen again, if only for a day."

"I think I'd pass. If I recall, sixteen had its own set of problems."

Millie chuckled. "You're right, dear, I'm sure. I believe my older brother was my main tormentor in those days." She gazed at the apple in her hand and suddenly remembered. "Say . . . I've been thinking, perhaps the secret is in the apples. Now, I know I've always used Granny Smith, but I was wondering . . . " She paused, faded blue eyes emanating unbridled excitement.

Vanessa laughed. The elderly woman's elation was contagious. A couple of months ago, she never would've imagined she could get this excited over *pie*. She'd been buried in the deepest despair of her life. It was a grief she just couldn't seem to overcome. Looking back, she realized her deep-seeded anguish was brought on by the fact that she had failed—at being a wife and mother, part of a family—and it was all her fault for the most part. She could've stayed with her ex for the sake of CJ. After all, the last half of their marriage was spent doing exactly that. Vanessa had remained faithful despite living with a stranger . . . until Alan came into her life. She fell in love, or so she'd thought, but it had been the biggest mistake of her life. She quickly discovered that when love was involved, the human brain stopped thinking logically. And Alan was in too big of a hurry, looking for things she wasn't ready or willing to give. He wanted to own her, tell her what to do and how to do it. *Was that love?* Regardless, it was like nothing Vanessa had experienced before, and she was disturbed to find she was willing to do anything he wanted, no matter what the cost to others. Thoughts of right and wrong flew out the window when they were together. There was a magnetic pull in their relationship, so consuming it was almost surreal. She'd become frightened at the sudden intensity and called it off, confessed everything to Bill, and then became a constant battering ram for his anger against the world. Since they'd been on a downhill slide anyway, it pushed their marriage over the edge.

In no time, Alan had moved on—their deep love for one another seemingly forgotten. Vanessa was alone—except for CJ, her reason for living . . . and Millie. God bless, Millie. The old woman never judged her, and not only offered advice, but had shown Vanessa family could mean many things, and simply having people who cared deeply for one another and held an interest in each other's well-being was what family was truly about. Millie was always sympathetic, yet stern when needed.

Millie played a significant role in CJ's life as well. With his father busy dating, twice in the past month he'd cancelled a weekend with his son. The kid had been devastated and Vanessa could see the pain hidden beneath the strong teenage rebellious front. When Millie found out, she had declared the day *Hot-fudge Sundae Sunday* and invited them over to watch Alfred Hitchcock's *The Birds* and eat massive amounts of ice cream. CJ had talked about it for days.

Guilt was heavy and came and went like a fickle lover, but as time went on, and with Millie's help, Vanessa was slowly recovering. She would never totally forgive what she'd done, lives she had ruined, hearts she had broken—her husband's, her son's, her lover's, her own.

It wasn't really *pie* that got Vanessa feeling giddy. It was Millie's friendship. This simple contest meant so much to the sweet aged woman—the tradition, the pride at making the best possible pastry— she deserved this honest accomplishment in her long, colorful life. And from what Vanessa had learned, it was indeed colorful. Her first husband was an award-winning novelist, but also bipolar and an alcoholic with a violent temper. His death was a suicide. Husband number two was more your average Joe, but fifteen years her senior and had a massive coronary while eating dinner at the local steak house. At the age of sixty-two Mildred Nelson had become a widow for the second time. She'd decided she wasn't going to bury a third, and spent the last twenty-five years concentrating on her children and grandchildren, babysitting, and baking.

Henry Baker had no idea the havoc he'd wreaked in Millie's life by winning the damn blue ribbon last year. Vanessa watched her friend obsess over each and every apple, divided by variety, and placed into groups on the kitchen counter. Perhaps she should pay Mr. Baker a visit, talk some sense into him . . . It was a baked goods contest for God's sake, and the holiday season—a time for giving. The man could bake anything. Why did he have to bake apple pie?

Millie turned, hands on hips. "So, young lady, are you ready to get to work?" She held out an apron.

Vanessa grinned and grabbed it, tying it snugly around her waist. "As always, Mildred Delores Nelson, I'm at your service."

Millie giggled like a school girl. She passed Vanessa a paring knife, and side by side they peeled apples, keeping the Honey Crisp separated from the Granny Smith as well as the Macintosh. "So, how are you today, dear? Did you sleep okay? You look a little peaked."

Vanessa brushed a random strand of copper hair from her eyes and tried to concentrate on not cutting off a finger along with the apple slices.

"I never sleep well . . . anymore." She shrugged. "Besides, there was a report I needed to finish for work."

Millie frowned. She worried about Vanessa. "You know what they say about all work . . . "

The two women peeled and talked, keeping the conversation light. Once the apples were peeled, and seasoned to perfection from pre-measured spices, they went to work on the crust. Millie's arthritic hands maneuvered the rolling pin like a pro, while Vanessa carefully centered each crust upon completion into a pie plate, mixing an exact amount of apple varieties with Millie's patient, guided instruction. The old woman topped each pie with a simple, yet elegant crust, fluting the edges expertly, then carefully placed them into the preheated oven.

While pies baked to a golden brown and the house filled with the heavenly aroma of apples and spices, the women drank coffee, and became lost in conversation until the timer startled them.

Donning oven mitts, Millie carefully removed each pie and set them on cooling racks.

Vanessa slipped her arm around Millie's narrow, stooped shoulders and squeezed. "They're beautiful, Mill."

"Well, looks can be deceiving as we both know." She turned a shrewd eye to the pies lined up in front of them. "The true test is yet to come."

Vanessa grinned. "That's the best part." They'd each have a piece and the remaining pie, plus two more would travel home with her.

"Oh! I know what I wanted to show you—the latest pictures of the grand-babies." She scampered off into another room as Vanessa refilled her coffee cup and sat at the kitchen table.

The cooling, fragrant pies brought back memories of her mother. She'd been gone almost five years now, but Vanessa missed her every day. Millie reminded her somewhat of the woman who had raised her; they tried to instill values and morals, but were never judgmental.

Millie returned with a pile of pictures and a proud-grandmother smile plastered on her wrinkled face.

They spent the next hour chatting and laughing at the crazy energy kids have as they perused each and every picture, reliving their own childhood through the photos.

Millie excused herself again, returning with a fine silver chain, intricate filigree cross hanging from the end. She passed it to Vanessa. "My mother's . . ."

"It's beautiful, looks almost antique." She had never seen such detail in so small a piece of jewelry. She handed it back, but Millie didn't take it—only shook her head and smiled, faded blue eyes moist with emotion.

"Try it on . . . here; let me help you, if my old arthritic hands will cooperate." She shakily clasped it around the young woman's neck, and then inspected her work. "Yes, beautiful." Millie radiated warmth and love. "I want you to have it, dear."

Vanessa placed her hand on the necklace around her throat. "Oh, Millie, I can't. It was your mother's. It should go to a family member."

"That's exactly right, dear. It should go to you. I think of you as a daughter . . . and friend. You mean a lot to me, Vanessa, and I cherish our time spent together. Merry Christmas." She touched the younger woman's hand, adding, "You make an old woman happy."

"With all my troubles . . . " Vanessa felt her eyes fill with tears. "It's *you* who's helped me." The two women hugged and softly cried.

"Okay . . . enough of this sniveling." Millie laughed. "It's pie time."

"My all-time favorite time." Vanessa grabbed a couple of small dessert plates from the cupboard, feeling at home, while Millie sliced into one of the pies.

She slid a plate of warm pie Vanessa's way, and grabbed a couple of forks from the silverware drawer.

"Ready-set-go," Vanessa offered with a broad grin. They cut into the pie simultaneously.

Millie frowned and chewed, deciphering and analyzing.

Vanessa gazed toward the ceiling, savoring every taste from tart to sweet to spicy. She looked at Millie, taking another forkful. "I think we have a winner, Ms. Nelson."

Millie blushed, took another forkful, and chewed. "You know . . . you may be right, dear. I do believe this is the best yet, a regular taste sensation. I knew it—the secret's in the apples."

"Well, now you know. You're sure to win, Millie. Henry Baker will simply have to settle for second place."

She smiled. "Yes, I think I finally have it in the bag." Seriousness crossed her features suddenly, and she leaned forward. "Tomorrow is the final day before the contest . . . and as you know, I must do it alone. I hope you understand, dear. No hard feelings?"

"Of course I understand! It's your own unique culinary creation. Just let me know if you need anything, okay? Call my cell. CJ and I will be at Mall of America doing some last minute Christmas shopping. The list seems to grow bigger every day."

"You're off all week, right? Are we still on for Thursday—day after tomorrow? She knew with Vanessa's hectic schedule, things could change at a moment's notice.

"I wouldn't miss it for the world, Mill. I'll pick you up at 8am. Judging starts at 9:00 sharp?"

Millie nodded, wringing her hands nervously. "Yes, 8:00 should be fine. Henry Baker was there before 6am last year, buttering up the judges." She shook her head, and then changed the subject. "I work the church dining hall for the annual Christmas dinner."

Vanessa rolled her eyes, wondering where the woman found the energy, and was still kicking herself for offering to help, although she knew it was the right thing to do. "Yep, me too . . . and CJ."

"Pastor Mattes will be so pleased to have us."

Vanessa nodded. "I know. It benefits everyone I guess . . . plus CJ still has a chance to hang out with his friends a bit beforehand at the carnival."

The women hugged and Vanessa left with an armload of pies, glad she only lived a couple of houses down.

CJ was on the living room couch with the dog, watching TV, still in boxers and a tee shirt. He hopped up and helped his mother unload her burden. "Man, I could get used to this." He didn't wait for an invitation, grabbing a knife and slicing a gigantic piece. Rufus, a beagle-terrier mutt they'd acquired after Bill left, followed the boy devoutly, hoping for a taste. Bill hated dogs. Rufus was now an important family member that had brought joy to both of them in the months since he'd moved in.

She handed CJ a plate and fork. "Let me know what you think, sweetheart."

"*Mmm,* good. Really good."

Vanessa looked up the Baker's telephone number and dialed, not sure what she'd say, but was greeted with a busy signal. "Can you hold down the fort a bit, kiddo? I won't be long, I promise. I need to pay someone a little visit."

CJ mumbled acknowledgement around a mouthful of sweet, juicy pie, while Rufus waited patiently for a crumb of the ever-so-flaky crust to be dropped.

<hr>

THE SNOW HAD LET UP A BIT AND the sun struggled to peek through. While cold, it was not unbearable. The five minute walk to the Baker's residence left Vanessa feeling exuberated as she rehearsed in her head exactly what she'd say. She turned up the drive, taking note of the freshly shoveled pavement and steps. He must have just done it. She remembered Henry telling her he had taken an early retirement. She'd run into him numerous times while walking Rufus. He seemed friendly enough. Rumor had it he was a burnout CEO of a large corporation. Lois, his secretary, had supposedly come along for the ride, and the money. Vanessa had yet to actually meet the Mrs. and would perhaps question if she even existed, except she'd seen them together at church. Lois was beautiful and not a day over thirty-five. She looked more like his daughter than his wife. To each his own, Vanessa thought as she raised her hand to ring the doorbell. She admired the beautiful wreath while waiting, lost in her own thoughts, then was quickly jolted out of her reverie when the door flew open, shocked by the words that assaulted her ears.

"What's the matter, bitch? Forget your toothbr—" Henry Baker stopped abruptly, seeing not his wife but a stranger . . . no, worse, a neighbor. *What was her name, Melissa? Clarissa?*

"Hi. Sorry to bother you. Vanessa Chandler," she offered, still recovering from his harsh words.

Henry blushed profusely. His wife was making him crazy, running around like a horny teenager. They were the talk of the town. It would be the death of him yet, he just knew it. He'd have a stroke, and then she'd take his fortune and run off with one of her young men. "I'm sorry. My wife . . . we were fighting and she left."

"No need explain." Vanessa smiled, returning her hand to her pocket, feeling extremely uncomfortable. "Been there, done that." She cleared her throat. "I was wondering if I could have a minute of your time."

Henry critically assessed her, eyes resting on her breasts briefly, and then met her gaze. "Certainly, please step inside. I have a pie in the oven."

Vanessa followed him. "Preparing for the baking contest?"

"Why, yes I am. I won the blue ribbon last year, and I plan to take it again this year. My pies are a work of art. My father was a pastry chef," he offered as way of an explanation.

"Funny you should mention that. That's why I'm here. Mr. Baker, I have an enormous favor to ask you." She noted the frown that creased his high forehead, seemingly making his bald head pucker, but forged ahead anyway. "My dear friend, Mildred Nelson, is eighty-seven years old. She has won a blue ribbon for her apple pie every year . . . except last year." She searched the man's face, hoping for a little compassion, but found none. "This is a *baking* contest . . . you could make *anything*—cookies, bars, fudge, peach pie, blueberry pie—just please, I beg you, don't make apple pie."

He smiled, sardonically. "My dear Miss . . . it is Miss, isn't it?"

Vanessa nodded, taking a step back, as he took a step closer.

"Miss Chandler. This is a free country. I am baking *apple* pie. Period. I will not be coerced into anything else. As for your friend?" The timer on the oven buzzed as if staged. Donning an oven mitt, he bent over to remove the pie.

Vanessa had a vision of planting her foot in his ass; send him crashing head-first into the hot oven. It wouldn't be that difficult being he was relatively small in stature. She shivered; kind of disturbed she could have such evil thoughts. But, he was a jerk.

Henry placed the perfectly browned pie, an intricate design etched masterfully into the crust, on the stovetop then turned to finish his statement. Gazing into the woman's jade green eyes, he offered simply, "May the best man win." He smiled at his choice of words, and then turned his attention back to the pie. It was perfection—a true masterpiece. The apple cut-outs and leafy vines he'd brushed with egg-white and sugar, sparkled invitingly. He turned to offer his guest a closer look, surprised to find the kitchen empty. Then he heard the front door slam, accustomed to the sound as of late. *Women—can't live with 'em.*

Vanessa walked home as fast as she could; dodging snowflakes, mad as hell. *What an ass. What a complete and total ass . . . But his pie—amazing.* She had a sick feeling in the pit of her stomach. She was afraid that once again Henry Baker would win the damn blue ribbon, leaving Mildred in the dust.

CJ was playing video games when she returned. He took one look at his mom and paused the game. "Hey, what's up? You look . . . frazzled."

Vanessa took a couple of deep breaths, suddenly hot. She peeled off her coat, hat, scarf and gloves. "I paid Millie's competition a little visit."

CJ's eyebrows shot up. "Henry Baker?" He was surprised. His mom usually tried to avoid confrontation at all costs.

"Yes. What a-a dickweed, to use your terminology."

He grinned. "Yeah, that's pretty much the consensus. He called the cops last month about the Langley's dog pooping in his yard." The Langleys' had a mutt that broke free and roamed the neighborhood periodically. Everyone just tolerated it. "And Tommy Driscoll lives right next-door. His cat disappeared and he's positive Henry Baker has something to do with it. The cat loved to poop in his well-groomed flowerbeds." CJ laughed. "Supposedly when ol' Henry was out weeding one day, he took his hat off and set it aside. When he went to put it back on, the cat had used it for a litter box."

Vanessa laughed. "I see a theme here—poop." Her laughter quickly faded.

CJ shook his head. "He seems kinda nutty to me. Tommy hates him, says he'd like to booby-trap his morning paper."

CJ and Tommy had been friends forever. Tommy was a year younger than CJ, but outweighed him by at least sixty pounds. *Big and slow*, was his nickname. Not the brightest bulb, he was nonetheless well liked and had been the neighborhood paper-boy, delivering the *Star Trib-une* to all the good folks on Johnny Cake Ridge for the past two years. No matter what the weather – rain, sleet, or snow, the kid got the paper out on time, his bicycle his only mode of transportation.

"His pies are something else though . . . a work of art." Vanessa looked at her son, slowly shaking her head.

"So, you think he'll slaughter Aunt Millie?"

Vanessa smiled at the familiar term the kid had tagged Millie with . . . she *was* a member of their family. "Well, let's just say it doesn't look promising, but we have to hope for the best. That's all we can do."

"Hey, cool necklace."

Vanessa touched her throat, forgetting for a moment the beautiful filigree cross that hung around her neck. "Millie gave it to me, it was her mother's."

"Wow. It's awesome. Hey, don't worry Mom. Millie's a tough one—a survivor."

"Yeah, aren't we all?" She ruffled his hair and went into the kitchen to see what she could rustle up for a quick supper, already thinking of a hot bath and an early evening.

AFTER A FITFUL NIGHT'S SLEEP, MILLIE woke way too early and couldn't fall back to sleep, despite warm milk and a short story in Reader's Digest. At 5am she decided to start the baking process, knowing from years past, she'd end up with enough pies for the entire neighborhood. She'd be bringing two pies for the contest—one for display and one for judging. She made a strong pot of coffee and at 5:15am slipped on her coat, opened the front door and stood on the steps. Like clockwork, here came Tommy, bag of papers slung over one shoulder, pedaling through wet snow and aiming, hitting the mark every time.

He arrived at Millie's and stopped. "Hey, Mrs. Nelson." He handed her the paper.

Millie smiled and placed a cellophane wrapped package into his paper bag. "Chocolate chip cookies," she said. She felt sorry for Tommy. He had lost his father several years ago in a work-related accident. A big kid for fifteen, he didn't hesitate to pick up the slack and help his mother make ends meet. In addition to the paper route, he unloaded trucks at the Farmer's Market in the summer and did odd jobs for pocket change. Everyone in the neighborhood liked him. "Here comes ol' Big and Slow" they'd say, and Millie would always correct them by saying, "His name is Tommy Driscoll."

Tommy grinned. "Chocolate chip are my fave. Thanks, Mrs. N. You're wicked awesome."

Millie blushed, despite the cold. "Wicked awesome—I like that. Let's hope the judges think so, too."

Tommy appeared confused for a moment, then nodded enthusiastically. "Oh yeah, that's right. Tomorrow's the big day, huh?"

Millie just smiled, nodding.

"My money's on you Mrs. N. You're the best cook in the world. Don't let anyone tell ya different. Just remember, wicked awesome." He climbed back on his bike, waving, and disappeared down the street.

Millie returned to the kitchen. Refilling her coffee cup, she sat at the table, and quickly skimmed the paper, thinking about Tommy and what a nice boy he was while she sipped the strong brew. *Wicked Awesome.* She had a good feeling—she'd get her mojo back this year and win that darn blue ribbon.

MALL OF AMERICA WAS crazy with last-minute holiday shoppers.

Vanessa thought of Millie as they milled through the crowd, and wondered how many pies were already baked and lined the counter. She had called her friend earlier and was greeted with a happy caffeinated voice. Everything was fine, she didn't need anything. Vanessa had promised to be there bright and early tomorrow morning.

Henry Baker was probably busy doing the same. Vanessa had driven past their house on the way to the mall this morning and noticed the garage open and Lois' car gone. She couldn't help but wonder if perhaps his charming wife didn't come home the night before or perhaps left early this morning to allow Henry ample room to exercise his baking prowess.

Piling everything into the back seat, they maneuvered the busy underground parking ramp, afternoon sun piercing the windshield when they emerged, blinking like moles.

"So, you ready for the big day tomorrow?"

CJ grinned. "Yeah, it's been a while since we've been to a carnival kinda thing together. I mean, ya know . . . Dad always hated anything with lots of people."

"I know. Not a real people person. Things change." She glanced at her son and smiled. "I think for the better—for the most part."

They drove in comfortable silence, satisfied and exhausted.

At least things were good with CJ. Vanessa had mixed feelings about tomorrow. A small miracle would need to happen. She fingered the cross Millie had bestowed upon her. *Please, God, let Millie win the blue ribbon this year.*

After a fitful night spent alone, Henry Baker strapped the cooler into the back seat as if it was a precious infant. The two pies nestled within were indeed a work of art—they belonged in the Smithsonian. He drove the dark morning streets to his final destination.

There were a couple of cars in the lot, so he'd likely be granted access into the building, and perhaps glean an opportunity to speak to the judges. Propping the car door with one hip, he reached into the backseat to unbuckle the cooler.

He never had a chance to react. Hit hard on the back of the head with bone crushing velocity, then again for good measure, bits of skull and brain fragment spattered as Henry Baker crumbled to a lifeless heap on the snow-covered ground, dead almost instantly.

The killer moved fast, dragging the body to the nearest street corner where a manhole cover lay partially open, waiting for the deposit. There was opportunity now and later, but at no time in between—too many people around both day and night due to the upcoming winter festivities. Quickly shoving Henry inside, the killer dropped the murder weapon on top of the body and slid the heavy manhole cover back into place, then jogged several blocks to where a getaway ride waited.

Vanessa arrived at Millie's house with CJ riding shotgun. The elderly woman was waiting patiently on the front step, pies carefully packed into a box, bundled up like an Eskimo.

CJ moved to the backseat, next to the pies, so Millie could sit up front and they drove to the community center in silence, each preoccupied with their own thoughts.

Vanessa pulled into the lot that accommodated both the community center and church being they shared common ground. She immediately spotted Henry Baker's car amongst several others which were now rolling in steady. He was already here. No doubt buttering up the judges as Millie mentioned he'd done last year. Sometimes life is such a bitch, she thought, sighing heavily, pulling into an open space near the entrance. She didn't want Millie stressed at walking too far. *Please, God . . .* Vanessa prayed her usual litany, hoping for once the big guy was listening. She looked over at her friend who appeared totally calm, cool and collected. She obviously hadn't noticed Henry's car. That was good. "So, Mill, we ready to rock and roll?"

Millie smiled broadly. "With the best of 'em, dear." She turned to CJ in the back seat. "Would you mind carrying the pies, son? It'd be just like me to drop them in a snow bank or something."

"Sure, no prob, Aunt Mill."

CJ begged to explore the carnival once he deposited the pies. Vanessa peeled off a twenty and sent him away.

. . . .

T HE CONTEST WAS READY TO BEGIN. Two long tables were lined with goodies, while judges sampled and talked amongst themselves. Millie and Vanessa sat near the front, and when one of the judges approached her pie, the old woman grasped Vanessa's hand so tight it hurt. He had a pleased look on his face after the taste-test. "That's a good sign . . . he's smiling," Vanessa whispered. She didn't see Henry's pies, and as she perused the crowd, saw no sign of Henry. *What's going on? Where's is he?* She looked at Millie who sat stoically, focused straight ahead, a small smile playing on her lips.

"We have the winners," a portly gentleman finally announced. He held several blue ribbons, and beginning at one end of the table, called out the winner's name, along with the item, ceremoniously placing the ribbon on the prized goodie. By the time he reached Millie's pie, Vanessa thought she'd internally combust with anticipation. "Mildred Nelson, apple pie."

Tears stood in Millie's eyes as she hugged Vanessa. "We did it," she whispered.

Vanessa smiled and gently patted her back. "No, Millie. *You* did it. I knew you would."

They hung out for a while talking and comparing notes with some of the other contestants. She took a picture of Millie holding her blue ribbon and another of the prize-winning pie, which would be placed in the display case for the duration of the festivities.

Vanessa half-expected Henry to come bursting through the door at any moment demanding to have his pie included, indignant and prissy, a wild story as to why he was detained, but he never showed.

Vanessa turned to Millie. "I bet you're pooped."

"No, actually I'm not. I'm thinking corn-dog, mini-donuts..."

Vanessa laughed. "You cannot be eighty-seven. You have more energy than me and I'm forty-five."

They donned coats, hats and all the Minnesota winter accoutrements, heading for the great outdoors and the carnival atmosphere.

"Ginseng, dear. That's the secret . . . and an ample amount of junk-food periodically. Anything in moderation," Millie offered as they followed a path shoveled through the snow, marked by large candy canes at regular intervals.

"I'll remember that . . . " Vanessa offered distractedly, taking in the amazing transformation of the church grounds.

In a daze she almost ran into a man who was looking everywhere but where she was. Millie was busy talking to a young woman with a baby on one hip. She watched the handsome stranger disappear into a make-shift gingerbread house.

Millie joined her and Vanessa described the familiar looking young man as they walked toward the ice sculptures.

"You should have pointed him out, dear. He sounds a lot like Edward Sills. He attends our church *and* . . . " Millie stopped, hating gossip.

"And . . . what?"

The two women walked slowly arm in arm, chatting about Lois Baker and Edward Sills. The talk around town was that they were having a not-so-clandestine affair. They were seen at some very public places together. Then their talk turned to Henry and the fact that he was missing in action.

"I saw his car when we pulled in," Millie confessed.

"Really? I never would've guessed it. You didn't appear nervous at all."

"I hide it well, dear. I've had a lot of practice. And besides, really, what was there to be nervous about? Winning wasn't up to me."

"Well, you won, fair and square. And I bet you'd still have that blue ribbon even if Henry had shown," Vanessa said with conviction.

"I am concerned, though. Henry must've gotten ill or perhaps had a pie mishap upon delivering them. I don't know. How can we find out?"

"You are so sweet, Millie. I tell you what, if his car is still in the lot when we leave, we'll take immediate action. If not, we'll play it by ear and at least talk to his wife, okay?"

Millie nodded, worry apparent in her usually merry blue eyes.

"Hey there's a place to sit and people-watch." She pointed to an open picnic table. "You sit, and I'll get junk food. What should we start with? Cheese curds, corn dog, mini-donuts," she read on the concession stand.

"One of each." Millie grinned. "Cheese curds for starters. And a Mountain Dew. I need the caffeine."

Vanessa got in line and ordered two cheese curds and two Dews.

Balancing curds in one hand, and sodas in the other, she almost lost it when she spotted the same tall, dark and handsome stranger again, walking toward the church. He turned the corner, probably on his way to meet Lois. She noticed her son walking hand in hand with a girl from school not far behind him. Now where was the kid going? He was on kitchen duty in half an hour.

After curds, they split a bag of mini-donuts, and then on Millie's insistence, walked the perimeter of the grounds before reporting for duty in the church dining hall to begin preparation for the annual Christmas dinner.

IN GOOD SPIRITS, THEY STASHED their purses and donned clean aprons. Tommy was busy peeling potatoes at a frantic pace, but CJ was nowhere to be found and wasn't answering his phone. Vanessa became madder by the minute, but tried to smile as she helped organize the chaotic kitchen. The dining hall was already filling up with people.

Even Millie was concerned, which made Vanessa more nervous. "He didn't answer his phone?" she questioned for the second time. The old woman had worry in her eyes, but the worry suddenly turned to surprise, and as Vanessa followed her line of vision, she too was left with mouth agape.

CJ had finally arrived, with two police officers in tow, entering the church kitchen uncertainly. The kid looked scared.

Vanessa quickly intercepted her son and his two uniformed friends at the kitchen entrance, wanting to avoid making a scene, which would be next to impossible considering work had virtually stopped and all eyes were on them.

"Hey, kiddo . . . what's up?" She stared at her son, then at the policemen.

"Can we step out in the hall, ma'am?" one of the officers asked.

"Certainly." She followed them into the hallway that separated the kitchen from the dining hall. What had CJ done now? He'd been through his share of trouble when their divorce was being finalized, but seemed to get it out of his system and there'd been no trouble since.

It was CJ that initiated the shock-wave. "They found Henry, Mom."

"Oh? Where was he? I bet he was upset about missing the contest . . . "

"He's dead!" CJ blurted out, tears springing to his eyes. "Sarah and I found his body when we were goofing around."

"What?" She looked at her son incredulously.

The cop who'd done all the talking so far, smiled thinly. "Your son wanted to show his girlfriend how strong he was, saw a manhole cover sitting off-kilter and hefted it off. Got more than he bargained for."

"Oh, my God! Dead?" Vanessa felt as if she'd been sucker-punched.

"Yes, very. Did you know Henry Baker?" The cop's eyes narrowed, assessing her demeanor.

"Yes . . . not well, but I knew him. We all did...neighbors." Her head was spinning. *Murder? Who would do this?* "Have you told his wife?"

The cop shook his head. "No, ma'am. She wasn't home. Do you know where we might find her?"

Vanessa nodded toward the church dining hall which was already half full. "You may want to check in there. Her um . . . friend was at the carnival earlier. I assume they'll be attending the dinner as well."

"Friend?"

"I don't know for sure." Vanessa didn't want to offer hearsay.

"I take it you'll be here awhile?" He looked from Vanessa to CJ and back to Vanessa.

"Yes, we start serving in an hour or so and then we're scheduled to clean up afterward."

The cop nodded curtly and motioned for his partner to follow, walking into the large dining room across the hall. They made their way to where Lois Baker and her lover, Edward Sills, sat deep in conversation, oblivious to everything around them.

Vanessa and CJ went in the opposite direction toward the kitchen and a waiting Millie.

• •

Lois and Edward departed with the two police officers, not knowing what had happened until they were riding in the backseat of a squad and were told they were being detained for questioning concerning the murder of Henry Baker.

Later that evening when prints from the murder weapon had been processed, they would both be booked for manslaughter and incarcerated.

Aᶠᵗᵉʳ ᴀ ʟᴏɴɢ ᴇxʜᴀᴜsᴛɪɴɢ ᴅᴀʏ, Vᴀɴᴇssᴀ and CJ dropped Millie off. "What a day, huh, Mill?"

The old woman nodded slowly. "It kind of makes the blue ribbon pie seem insignificant. Henry dead . . . hard to believe." She wiped a single tear from her eye, and smiled sadly at Vanessa. "Thanks for everything, dear."

"We'll talk tomorrow. Try to get some rest, okay? Call me if you need *anything*."

Millie nodded acknowledgment and shuffled slowly up the walkway.

Vanessa worried; the old woman had been through a lot today. She waited until Millie got through the front door, and then drove the short distance home.

Mɪʟʟɪᴇ ᴘᴏᴜʀᴇᴅ ᴍɪʟᴋ ɪɴᴛᴏ ᴀ ᴄᴜᴘ ᴀɴᴅ placed it into the microwave for one and a half minutes, added a dash of brandy, then settled into her rocker. She sipped and thought . . . *There will be extra cookies for Tommy when he delivers the morning paper. He's anything but big and slow. He's loyal and trustworthy and will do anything for a friend . . .*

Tommy had been told by a little bird what time Henry would be at the community center.

Three days ago, Edward Sills changed a flat tire after dropping Lois off. Not having a crow bar, he'd borrowed one from the Baker's garage, accounting for his and Lois' fingerprints on the murder weapon.

Big and slow Tommy remembered to wear gloves without being told a second time.

Millie smiled. *Life is what you make it. It can be a bitter pill to swallow . . . or sweet as pie.*

Camille Hyytinen lives in Waterville and writes edge-of-your-seat crime thrillers based in Minnesota. Hyytinen's first novel, *Pattern of Violence,* depicts a homicidal maniac on the streets of Minneapolis. The second in the Maria Sanchez Thrillers series, *Pattern of Vengeance,* picks up years later, with deadly results. Hyytinen continues the storyline in an anthology, *The Heat of the Moment—Where There's Smoke . . .* Camille is currently working on several new projects.

For Want of Some Gloves

Barbara DaCosta

OB THE BUS DRIVER PULLED UP to the bus shelter in his north-bound Number 18 bus. He tapped impatiently on the steering wheel as people got off.

Everything was running late, typical for Christmas-time. Got all this snow and ice, then you've got your riders with bulky coats carrying all kinds of packages. But today, all he cared about was that he was running late and he really wanted to use the bathroom. He'd have just enough time for that before returning southbound.

Bob distracted himself by looking at the department store windows. He'd have to bring the wife down this weekend to see the Christmas decorations. She always liked seeing them and the bell-ringers. " 'Tis the season," she always reminded him when he grumbled too much.

In any case, life could be worse, much worse. There's that homeless guy again by the bus shelter. Tattered green ski jacket. Just sitting in the snow on the granite lip of the boarded-up-for-winter fountain, begging for handouts. Poor guy.

AS THE NUMBER 18 BUS PULLED UP, Terrence stuck his weather-beaten hands back into his pockets to warm them for a brief moment. He hated panhandling, but with a bum back and bum eye, there wasn't much work he could get. His right eye still wasn't working so well. Two years ago, the doctor said to get surgery, but the company wasn't about to pay for that—and he lost the job, anyway.

Man, sure was cold out. Snow and more snow. Five months of it. Minne-snow-ta, they oughta call this place. November wind howling down from the North Pole and he was still without gloves. Fingers almost frozen. Maybe he could panhandle enough today to get a pair. Could head down to the thrift store later on, see what they have. That's where the green ski jacket and purple stocking cap had come from. But best for now to sit tight here by the bus shelter and try to beg more money. Bus riders are always more sympathetic. They know what it's like to be outside in the winter.

Terrence's jeans had a tiny hole over one knee. The wind was like a hot-cold needle piercing through that hole right into his very soul. He adjusted the one-inch-thick sheaf of corrugated cardboard beneath him, the only significant barrier between his derriere and the cold edge of the covered-up fountain.

"Der-ri-ere," that's what Aunt Sofia used to call it, back in New Orleans. She'd always draw the word out. He once said "b-u-t-t" in front of her, and never heard the end of that. Still could taste the soap in his mouth from that one. Aunt Sofia sure was a proper, upright woman.

Terrence stuffed his hands further into his pockets in a vain search for warmth.

***

Donald readied to exit from the rear door of the northbound Number 18 bus. Dressed in a spotless camel-hair coat, a blue-and-yellow plaid scarf around his neck, and with a pair of well-polished shoes, Donald tugged his hand-made, fur-lined, imported leather gloves on a little tighter. His medium-brown hair was carefully trimmed and combed. He had slight splotches of red on his pale cheeks.

It was absolutely important to look successful. That was one of Donald's Rules for Life. Always look good, always act confident. Then, people trust you. Like Jennifer. With one smile from Donald, she was hooked.

Time to get her a nice Christmas gift, something to demonstrate how their relationship had grown. Then, she'd for sure want to reciprocate—like with an invitation to join her at her condo in Hawaii for New Year's.

Donald tugged once more on his finely made gloves. He peered through the window of the bus door before pushing it open. He could see an old black guy sitting on a street fixture, panhandling. He was slouched over, wearing a ratty green ski jacket and purple knit hat. Looked defeated. No confidence. No wonder people were walking right by him without even a glance. Pretty sorry situation if a man can't even manage to hustle money from people at Christmas-time. As Donald stepped down from the bus to the pavement, an idea came to him.

"Spare some change?" Terrence asked, putting out his bare hand as the passengers from the Number 18 walked by. This young white guy with the plaid scarf looked promising. In a good mood about something. Nice threads. About thirty-five years old.

"Spare some change, sir?" Terrance looked up, hand extended, at the young man.

"Well, actually, yes," said the young man. "Someone just gave me an awesome gift. I want to spread the holiday cheer and help someone else in turn. Got ten bucks here with your name on it."

Terrence gave the young man the once-over before answering. "Alright," he said. Ten dollars wasn't something to pass up.

"You need something in particular?" the young man from the bus asked. "I could take you to the department store."

"I gotta get me some gloves. It's cold out here," answered Terrence.

"Come on, then. I'll buy you a pair of gloves."

They crossed the street, like new best friends, to the department store, the one with the fancy Christmas displays.

"By the way, my name's Donald," the young man from the bus said as they approached the doors of the store, passing the Salvation Army bellringer.

"I'm Terrence."

"Where are you from, Terrence?"

"Louisiana."

"You like it up here?"

"It's fine. Just too cold. Too cold for these old bones." Terrence had started calling himself old just a couple of years ago, even though he was just fifty-three.

Life itself was making him feel stiff and old.

WHEN DONALD AND TERRENCE ENTERED the department store, Terrence's eyes couldn't help but widen—it'd been years since he'd been in a store this fancy. Big, beautiful, clean, warm. Holiday decorations on every wall. Colors splashed all over like a tropical forest. Wide, maroon-carpeted aisles. A live piano player under a tall Christmas tree. The intoxicating scent of leather and perfume. Everything and anything for sale: knit scarves, silk ties, gold jewelry, stylish clothing, crystal and china, dress shoes—you name it.

Terrence had forgotten how clean and orderly things could be. Just how life should be, even if his own wasn't at present.

Aunt Sofia had preached that to anyone who stood still long enough. Clean, orderly. Self-pride. How you present yourself to the world counted, especially if you were black.

"Child, they'll use any excuse to keep you back, so you've got to carry yourself well." Aunt Sofia had raised Terrence after his mother had died. But Aunt Sofia died four years prior, and since losing his job two years ago, Terrence's life had slipped out of control. He'd had some low-pay work, but then lost it, and was now sleeping on his friend Daumants' couch.

It tore him up to go against everything Aunt Sofia had taught him, but he had no choice. No job. No home. Couldn't even get into a government program. No place to go, not even for the holidays.

As the two men looked for the glove department, Donald's head was filled with warm fantasies. Jennifer's blond hair, fine figure, and nicely tanned skin. Her perfect smile. They'd met two months ago at a bar downtown. Hawaii was where her tan had come from, she'd said with a tinkling laugh and toss of her hair. Her job in upper-level corporate management had gotten her the condo in Waikiki. Gold jewelry gleamed as they chatted.

He'd smiled back at her, coyly. Things had moved along nicely since then.

Very nicely.

Now it was time for the next move.

AFTER FINDING TERRENCE A PAIR OF $10 imitation-leather synthetic-fleece-lined gloves, the two men rounded the corner by the jewelry department.

"Hold up a minute, Terrence, I want to look at something for my girlfriend for Christmas," said Donald. They stopped by one of the brightly lit glassed-in displays of glittering, shiny baubles. A saleslady stood behind the counter.

"May I look at those?" Donald pointed at some gold hoop earrings in the case. Some modest-priced ones hung on a countertop rack, but they wouldn't do.

The saleslady smiled. Bending over, she used a key to open the case, and reached in to extract the jewelry. She straightened up and laid the earrings on the glass countertop. The price tag read $300.

Perfect, Donald thought to himself. He took his time examining the gold earrings.

Further down the counter, Terrence gazed at the watch display. He'd always wanted a gold watch. Aunt Sofia had said he could have Grandpa's gold watch after she was gone, but it had disappeared many years ago when she was having the house painted. Terrence knew the gold watches in the glass case would be far too expensive to even dream about, but these imitation ones on top of the case . . . they couldn't be too expensive, if he saved up over this next year. He reached toward the watches that hung from a wooden display rod.

Donald, from a few feet away, kept an eye out as Terrence stretched out his hand to touch the watches. At the moment that the saleslady turned her head to look toward Terrence in his ratty clothes, Donald casually but quickly slipped the pair of gold earrings into one of his leather gloves and substituted a cheaper, similar pair of earrings from the display rack on the counter. In the blink of an eye, the deed was done.

Terrence wiggled his shoulder in his jacket—his skin was itching. He squirmed around to try and relieve it. Man! So hot in this store. What was with these northerners? It's ten degrees outside, can't they see everyone has heavy coats on? No, they had to go heat the place up hotter than a desert in July. Terrence reached inside his jacket. Ahh! Yeah, there's the itch.

"Sir? Excuse me." A uniformed security guard appeared out of nowhere, full of youthful authority. "Could you place your hands out in front of you, please."

Terrence groaned. He knew better than to argue. He'd been up north long enough to know the routine. He was WWB—Walking While Black. Even worse, Walking While Black and Homeless in a fancy department store. Doesn't matter that he hadn't done nothing except scratch an itch. Just gotta do like Aunt Sofia always told him, be polite, do what you're asked to do. Don't argue.

The saleslady stood stock-still, one hand still holding the display case key, while the security guard steered Terrence by the elbow towards the back offices.

Donald, gripping his leather gloves, knew from experience that Terrence would be hung up for at least an hour in the security office being searched and questioned before they'd realize that he hadn't done anything except look out of place.

The saleslady was totally unaware of how Donald slowly backed away from the counter and entered the flow of holiday shoppers, disappearing into the crowd.

Donald briskly strode through the store, past the piano player and the Christmas tree, his spotless camel-hair coat flapping with his stride, a smirk on his face.

Hot damn! Jennifer was really going to dig these earrings! She'd get all gushy and insist on taking him to Hawaii, for sure. Once he was there—yes! It'd be clear sailing. He'd easily be able to insinuate himself further into Jennifer's glamorously rich life. These earrings were going to be his ticket into the big bucks!

Donald pushed open the Seventh Street door, the stolen earrings still hidden in one of his gloves. He'd be home in fifteen minutes on the bus, at most. Plenty of time to wrap up these babies, call Jennifer to make a date, and—

Blustery cold air hit Donald full force in the face. Icy spicules of snow made him blink. His foot hit a patch of ice and in an instant, he slipped, falling face-first onto the snowy pavement. His handmade leather gloves flew out of his grasp through the air, falling with their hidden treasure into the dirty, slush-filled gutter, where they landed right in front of the big, heavy, rolling wheels of the southbound Number 18 bus.

Barbara DaCosta's debut children's book *Nighttime Ninja*, illustrated by award-winning artist Ed Young, will be out from Roaring Brook Press in late 2011. She is at work completing her novel *Death by the Depot*. DaCosta's "Cabin 6" appeared in the *Resort to Murder* anthology published by the Minnesota Crime Wave.

Plant You Now, Dig You Never

Joan Murphy Pride

MY FATHER WAS USUALLY A PUSHOVER for anything I cared to tell him, which made my teen years hell. I couldn't lie to such a sweet man so it kept me from doing anything dangerous, unlawful or even faintly interesting. Now, for the first time, he wouldn't believe my story. And this could be a matter of life and death. Mine.

Mom didn't believe me either when I told her she was living next door to two murderers because these men were her latest cause. She lived to fight prejudice and when the two "nice boys," as she called them, moved in next door, she took them under her benevolent wing. They couldn't have found a better front.

Mom summoned me to a Christmas party to welcome the new neighbors. When her phone call started with "Amy Emma Connolly" I knew I'd have to be there. Tonight they'd meet the Connolly family. We all love to come home. My mother is a woman with missions you might not want to join but she really can cook.

And the family home, overlooking Lake Harriet, is the perfect Christmas house, with white brick and turrets on the third floor and candles in every window.

I opened the front door, went into to the hall and hung up my mammoth goose down parka. I stopped to admire the tree, a huge and gorgeous pine that climbs two stories to the balcony on the second floor. It was decorated with so many ornaments, and every one was a part of all my wonderful Christmas memories in this house.

I yelled, "Hey, Toots, where are you? I'm ready to eat."

No answer but I could smell something delicious so I knew she was close about and cooking. I meandered next into the den, looking for my father. I could always count on him being there at six p.m., watching the news and swearing softly.

His face brightened when he saw me. He said, "Hello, Princess. I'm glad to see you, Honey. I hope you're staying home for the holidays."

"Yes, my dear parental unit, I am here for a week," I said. "Tell me how many misunderstood citizens you sent to the slammer today? Is there a chance one of them could be a triple, maybe even a serial murderer? Hand over some inside dope."

Dad's a judge and there wasn't a chance I'd get anything out of him I couldn't read in the *Star-Tribune*, but I kept trying. I'm interested in crime and have always known I'd make a super detective. You know, like Miss Marple, only lots cuter and younger. I did solve a double murder last winter at the Birkebeiner Race, which was great. But it had cost me my advertising copywriter job, moving to London with Ryan Kelly, my One True Thing, and very nearly my life. Why wallow in the past? I was ready to have another go at crime. And this time I'd be careful, have a foolproof plan, stay totally safe and be really brilliant.

"Amy, you'll never guess what your Mother is doing now."

I leaned over the back of his chair and ruffled my Dad's snow-white hair. "What now? Is it civil disobedience, resisting arrest, blockading traffic, or chaining her body to something? Don't worry. You know she's tough as an old boot."

"No, it's nothing dangerous this time. But it's worse. She's running for City Council on a Gay Rights ticket. She's out speaking everywhere and she wears a t-shirt that says, '*I can't even think straight*'. I don't even know what means."

I laughed. My Mom is the patron saint for anyone she feels isn't getting a level playing field from society. She's politically correct in every way one can be-- religious, racial, sexual. She's carried the flag for the disabled, elderly discrimination, mental illness, immigration and even rights for nutty fringe groups. But this is the first time she'd run for office. I had to go see the candidate for myself.

I banged into the kitchen, found my mother and said, "You rang and issued an order for me to be here for dinner tonight, Toots?"

"I've asked you a million times not to call me Toots, Amy. And while we're discussing your idea of a great joke, please tell me why you're dressed like a combination vagrant and tart."

"I am hurt," I said, "and furthermore these heavily distressed jeans are from a famous designer and cost more than anything I've bought all year. You're in luck though, Kiddo. I brought a full suitcase of clothes and you can pick the outfit of your dreams for me to wear to dinner. Just pretend I'm your own large Barbie Doll."

"Toots? Kiddo?" said Mom. "What are you, a leftover from the nineteen-twenties? And why did your bring a full suitcase? I'm going to use your old room as my campaign headquarters. I don't remember inviting you and, no, you cannot move back in again. So skidoo kiddo."

"I have to move back for awhile. The furnace in my building is out again. It's just for a few days, and you can use my room for your meetings too, as soon as I get up."

"Amy, my meetings start early. You'd better be gone by 7:30 A.M. each morning or be prepared to meet strangers in your nightgown."

"Mom, I don't wear anything to bed. I go native. Your staff will see the totally adorable Amy."

Mom laughed. "Wear whatever you want or nothing at all. We'll be there at seven-thirty. And I expect to see something decent on you tonight."

"I promise. I'll change to something really nice I got at a charity sale that looks very expensive and matronly. Who's coming anyway? Crowned heads? Dad's fellow judges? Or the really important people, Bennett and Carter?"

Mom's face softened at the mention of her adored grandchildren. "They'll be here, of course, and all the rest of the family too."

That included my oldest brother, Police Detective Mike, his funny and fun wife, Kath and their little boys; my middle brother, Father Kevin, a Catholic priest; and last, my youngest brother Fitzgerald or Fitz. He's a highly successful, very expensive lawyer. He'll bring a date, the latest in his series of stunning beauty queens.

I'm the youngest and all my brothers believe they have a duty to co-parent me.

"We're having a dinner party," Mom continued, "to introduce the family to our wonderful new neighbors, Jim and Derek. They are such nice boys and wonderful partners for each other. They've been through a lot of prejudice. They're a little insecure grammatically and socially but really fine young men who are very happy together."

"Ah," I said, "I'm beginning to see the reason for your running for office."

Mother sighed. "I want to help them feel wanted in the neighborhood."

"Why wouldn't they?" I said, "This is one of the friendliest and most accepting neighborhood in Minneapolis."

Evening came, the whole family gathered. It was loud and fun and happy as always. Then the two new neighbors arrived, ill at ease and dressed in jeans and wrinkled, white shirts with loud Christmas ties. Jim had a tie that kept blinking off and on, too. Derek's conversation was limited but I tried my best to find out everything I could about him.

I didn't get very far when Derek gave me a look, black as his permanent five-o'-clock-shadow and said, "What's with the questions, kid?"

Big Jim, as Derek introduced him, was giving me piercing glances too, but of a quite different kind.

I was getting a funny feeling that maybe these two nice young men weren't the real goods. They talked funny and were trying to act posh, but both came out phonier than Fitz's date's boobs.

Their clothes were weird for men who could afford a house on a city lake. These bozos wore outfits straight out of a dumpster dive. I had a feeling they were scamming my Mom and I wanted to know why. I could see why she would be useful to them. If they searched the whole state of

Minnesota, they couldn't have found a better or more credulous next-door neighbor.

I took the remains of the first course, cream of leek and spinach soup, out to the kitchen. As soon as the swinging door shut behind me, I said softly, "Those guys are not gay, Mom. Neither one of them is gay."

"Oh, Amy. Don't start. Of course they are."

"No, they're trying to act gay. They're just playing a role."

"Why would they claim to be something they're not? What in the world would they get out of that?"

"That's the big enchilada, isn't it Mom? What are they after?"

She didn't answer my question but went on attack, instead. She accused me of knowing nothing about gay culture. This was totally unfair as two of my closest friends are a gay couple, Peter Andrew and his partner Mark Rollings.

I knew better than to argue. Mom had marched at the Gay Pride Parade at Loring Park. She'd bought a wardrobe of tee shirts with slogans that showed her solidarity. She adopted Big Jim and Derek and was busy making them a part of our family. Which is why later I, Amy Connolly, was sitting in my folk's dining room being felt up under the table by Big Jim.

He pretended to give me a little pat and then slowly started up my leg towards my Forbidden Citadel. I turned and smiled at him and reached under the tablecloth and grabbed his little finger. I bent it back so far, I heard it crack. And everyone heard his cry of pain, which he attempted to explain was due to a terrible cramp. I didn't hear his finger break, though. Pity.

The evening was not a big success in spite of the fact that the Connollys were all madly trying. They weren't getting much back from the next-door nice boys. Derek offered his opinion that dinner had been great grub. Big Jim said 'awesome' or 'enchanting' every other minute.

When the conversation ground to a complete halt, nine-year-old Bennett felt the need to step up.

"Wanna hear a great joke?" he said. We all agreed a good joke was just what the party needed.

"Why did the goldfish cross the road?" We all shook our heads indicating we hadn't a clue, so he continued. "Because the chicken had the day off." He chortled loudly and we all joined in with gusts of laughter, high fives for Bennett and hugs from his Nonna. Not a glimmer from the two nice boys. They looked bored.

From the other side of the table came the pounding on the table of a milk glass. "I have a joke, too," said Carter. He's six years old. We begged him to tell us his joke. He stood up on his chair to say, "Why does a duck have big feet? To stamp out forest fires."

By now Carter was so overcome with giggles, he could hardly finish.

He continued "Why does an elephant have big feet? To stamp out burning ducks."

That's a great joke, I thought. So was Bennett's. Everyone was laughing and making a fuss over Carter but not our guests. They looked sullen and disgusted.

When Carter looked at them, his little face fell and he looked sad. I wanted to go over and kick those guys on that perfect target for women wearing Manolo Blahniks.

I got up instead and said, "Well, look at the time! It's pretty late on a school night for my adorable, smart and very funny nephews."

Luckily, my brothers got the hint and all stood up, forcing the two child haters to get up too. I got their coats so fast they were at the front door before they knew where they were headed. Derek shook hands with everyone. He had ground-in dirt on his hands and what looked like black dirt under his fingernails. Big Jim air-kissed my mother and gave her a little hug. Then he turned to me and hugged me like a large boa constrictor.

He murmured in my ear, "You da bomb, kid. You da bomb."

This was bad enough but what came next was hideous. I could feel something poking me. I knew this was Big Jim's disgusting way of showing his approval of my bomb of a body. I pushed him away and tried to get my knee in place to finish him off but I was too late and he just laughed. The whole unsavory scene started my finicky stomach's gag reflexes with belches that I'm sure everyone heard.

I knew for a scientific fact that these non-gay gays were phony, from their ape-like heads to their smelly feet. And now I also suspected they were crooked. There had to be a really good reason for their pretense. Well, whatever it was, they weren't going to hurt another member of my family. I'd find out what they were up to and get rid of them.

The next morning I got up early and made my bed, two foreign moves for me.

I grabbed one of my old U of M notebooks and headed for coffee. I sat down at the kitchen table with my dad who was reading the paper and swearing softly. I didn't disturb him. Children shouldn't try to change a parental unit's habits. They're too old to change and, trust me; they won't thank you for trying.

I started a list of everything I could do safely to discover what the new neighbors were up to. I knew I couldn't just go next door for a drop-in visit. That was sure to end with Big Jim doing something to me that would force me to hurt him. And I could hurt him. I'm only five-feet-three-and-a-half but my brothers taught me how to fight and while I was often bloodied, I was never bowed.

I needed to get the dirt on the neighbors in a more civilized manner. Total surveillance would be one, really safe way. I needed to watch them twenty-four-seven, and track all visitors and deliveries. And there were lots of both. Just this morning I had counted five cars and two trucks with workers carrying in bag after heavy bag of something. When I sleep I might miss action that would start me on the right path to their removal. I was going to need help.

Mom told me that Derek Cranowski was a very successful financial planner and that his clients met with him at his house. Only my mother would believe this. Whatever Dirty Derek was handing out next door, it wasn't a legitimate way to make money.

My lifetime squeeze, Ryan Kelly, also my husband-to-be when I'm older and ready to quit flirting with other guys, was in London. He'd be home soon for the Christmas holidays and I can get him to do anything with me, but I was hot to get going now.

I made a list of my closest friends but I feared all of them would say no.

A few tiny problems had arisen for them during my last case, the murders at the Birkebeiner. My pals are still wallowing in grudges. Well, nothing much lost, the wimps. But I would have to use my brothers. This would also be tricky, as I have occasionally burned them over the years. But they'd have to help. I'd use family love and lots of guilt.

Brother Mike, a Minneapolis police detective in the 5th Precinct, was my obvious choice. He had all that great cop stuff like x-ray photography, listening bugs, and tough guys to smash down doors. But I knew Mike didn't want me anywhere near his office.

I went down to his precinct anyway but before I could sneak in and sit down, Mike just marched out and headed me toward the door.

"Amy," he said, "I love you like a sister. Now go home."

"I need you to help me get rid of those phony morons next door. It would be so easy for you," I started to ask.

"Forget it. Nothing with you is easy. Your last little plan almost got me put on report. Goodbye."

"You're getting old, Mike. Creaking as a matter of fact. And surly, horribly surly," I said as I left.

Well, next on the list was my number two brother, Father Kevin. The last protest of my anti-war group hadn't gone too well at his church. I'm pretty sure there were men in uniforms there at the end but I'd been in a hurry to get out the lady's room window so I could be wrong. I moseyed into Father Kevin's office and asked for help.

"Never, never again," my godly brother said in a truly belligerent tone of voice. "The last time you and your nutty friends were here protesting, it got me in a lot of trouble."

"Ah," I said, "that sounds like my old Kevin, the one that used to whack me with regularity. But I must say, it lacked a certain charity one expects from a priest."

He swallowed hard. "You're right, but remember you and your troops came in dressed as wounded soldiers, all bandaged and with lots of phony blood. One was on crutches, another, supposedly dead, being pushed on a gurney. Every child in the congregation is still having bad dreams nightly."

"Little sissies."

"And I was called to see the Bishop. I am not getting involved in anymore of your weird theater. Go away. I don't want you within three city blocks of my parish."

"Well, I can see you've lost the great love you had for worthwhile causes and fellow humans. You're a hollow shell now, Kevin."

He didn't whack me as he muscled me out. He did something meaner. As he said goodbye to me at the door, he raised his hand in blessing and said, "I'll pray for you, little sister."

One last chance to find brotherly love. That was Fitz, my youngest brother and he would be easy. He thinks I'm funny, never gets mad, just ruffles my hair and offers to sue anyone I want sued. I was escorted in to his posh offices, first by an incredibly gorgeous guide, who eyed me coldly like I was competition. Next came a long–legged, bored brunette who is Fitz's planner and finally to Miss Angelina, who does all the real work.

"I'll take you right in, Amy, but you have just five minutes. Our boy is very busy today." This is a woman who needs a life, I thought. And some sex, great sex.

Fitz started laughing before I even got all the way in.

"Whatever you want, Sprout, it's yours."

"Well, I need your good camera with the long lenses. The one that dates each shot. And your voice-activated tape recorder."

"You got them. I'll buzz Miss Angelina and tell her to package them up. Incidentally, are you borrowing them or is this visit going to cost me plenty? And what's the trouble? We can fix it."

"I'm not in trouble, Fitz, I just need help spying on the baddies next door."

"Nope. No help here Sprout."

"Why? You never say no to me."

"You never threatened my license to practice law before. Spying is an illegal act for the average citizen. The government, of course, does it all the time, usually unnecessarily, which is why I'm so rich. I can't do it. I'm going to assume you don't plan to use my camera and tape recorder for anything but happy Christmas memories. If you aren't, don't tell me."

I patted his hand. "Poor dear old Fitz. You've become as mushy as your blonde bimbo's over-peroxided hair."

He laughed. "She's not so dumb, Amy. Are you leaving right after the holidays for the French Polynesian Islands?"

He buzzed for Miss Angelina. She took my elbow to hustle me out, and I must say that little old lady has a mean grip. I drove back to my folks quite bummed. I could think of no reason on earth God would have given me the hell of three nosey, bossy brothers if they wouldn't help me when asked.

Then I had a brilliant thought. I could get Mom to help me if she didn't know what I was really doing. So I hurried home happier. Mom was having a meeting in the library so I headed for the kitchen and started making chocolate chip cookies. It's the only thing I know how to make from scratch.

When Mom joined me, she was immediately suspicious. "What are you up to, Amy? It's not like you to hang around baking cookies."

"How sharper than a serpent's tooth is an untrusting Mother. These cookies aren't for me. They're for the boys next door to apologize for my doubts about them."

My mother looked a tad embarrassed. "Why, Amy. How sweet of you. How unlikely but really, how sweet."

"It is sweet, isn't it?" I said smugly. "But to be honest I'm dying of curiosity. What are they doing to that nice old house?"

"I'm curious too. They must be replacing everything. Can I take the cookies over with you?"

My cookie plot had worked. The neighbors would have to let me in with Mom along. We got to the front door, rang the doorbell and spooky old black-bearded Derek opened the door. He nodded to Mom and turned to me.

"Whadda you want, kid? We ain't got it."

Mom looked surprised at his roughness but I wasn't. This man was a thug. I just smiled and said, "We thought we'd bring you some cookies, fresh from the oven."

Derek turned back to Mom and said, "Sorry I can't let you in ma'am. Big Jim would kill me. He doesn't want anyone to see it until it's all, ya know, decorated good."

Mom smiled, shook his filthy paw and turned around and left. Derek grabbed the cookies from me and tried to close the door. But I'm quick and got there with my foot first. The door swung open wide enough so that I could see all the front hall and part of the living room. The expensive and beautiful French wallpaper was hanging down in strips everywhere and it looked damp, very damp. There was an odd smell, too.

Derek snarled, "Look. Get your big foot out of my door. I'm busy and Big Jim is gone. Which you better hurry up to be."

With that, footsteps could be heard climbing the stairs into the kitchen. Big Jim appeared on the top step. He was yelling to Derek. "Get your ass down in that basement. I can't do it all alone. You're not paying me enough."

"Shut up. That girl from next door is here."

"Ah," Big Jim said as he came to the door. "The body beautiful. C'mon Amy. Let's go into the backyard or out for a nice ride and have some personal time together."

He grabbed my arm and I was getting nervous. I could see Mom turning into her house. I knew they couldn't kill me because she knew where I was, but Big Jim might do things to me I'd need to kill him for.

I tried to squirm away but didn't work so I thought I'd give Jim a little warning.

"You'd better let me go. I know you're not gay. I might have to blow your cover."

His face went blank. "And then I'd have to blow you away for good."

Okay, now I was scared. "Big Jim, can't you take a little joke? I came over today because I thought, well noticed, you kind of like me, that's all I meant. Let me go please. Mom's waiting. We can get together later."

He let me go but I could see he wasn't entirely sure about me. I had gotten some information, but I had been terrified. I noticed Jim had hands and arms like a boxer so he wasn't just another pretty face. He was a thug, just like his partner.

I raced home. I needed a partner to keep me safe. Where was Ryan? He was supposed to be home over the weekend for Christmas and now it was almost Wednesday. I went home and, as though I had wished him up, Mom was holding the phone out to me. "It's Ryan, dear. Wait until you hear what he's been doing. It's like a movie or a book by Ngaio Marsh. Super fun."

I grabbed the phone and said, "And what fun have you been having," I said in my chilliest voice, "instead of rushing to the arms of the woman you profess to love?"

"Amy, lovey, how I wished you were with me. I was invited for a real weekend in the country and it was like a movie. A stately home, full or art with hundreds of rooms. It looked like Darcy's from that movie you're so gooey about."

"Jane Austen's *Pride and Prejudice*."

"It was really an incredible weekend from Friday noon to Monday afternoon. A banking weekend, you know."

"One of the British guys in your new office?"

"No, actually a barrister from the Big Ben Insurance Company. Lady Ann. She's the daughter of the Earl of Essex. Very peppy, lots of fun. You'd love her."

I doubted it with all my jealous heart but I wasn't going to tell Ryan that. I just told him what the problem was, what I was doing and that I needed him to keep me safe while I was doing it.

Ryan said, "I'm coming to your folks for dinner tonight. We can go out after and you can show me how much you've missed me in truly meaningful ways. Then we'll figure those hoods out together. Let's, ah, see if we can find some legal ways to stop them though, okay?"

Everything was great as soon as Ryan and I touched. After dinner we had a fabulous evening doing this and that in my frozen apartment, the only place we could be alone. All of Ryan's siblings were home for Christmas, two with babies. My family was underfoot constantly and my Dad's fussy sister and my Mother's favorite aunt, Sister Patricia, had moved in for the holidays.

"Don't go to the dark side, Amy," Ryan said, "Christmas is Saturday, and on Monday we'll head for a luxurious and very private cabin on Lake Superior."

"Wonderful Ryan. But there will be no skiing. None."

He laughed, "You might like it there, lovey. It's flat as a banker's ass along the shore. It's great exercise but maybe we won't need more exercise."

Ryan took me back to my parents and I thought how to get the bad guys out before Monday. I knew there was only one way to do that. I had to get into their house and down into the basement. That's where the real action must be going on.

I was almost totally convinced at this point that they were making Methamphetamine. I knew it was easy to make with do-it-yourself instructions right on the Internet. Trouble was, Meth could be tricky for dummies and often it blows up. If the boys' house exploded and burned down, so might my parents! I had to stop them.

They didn't seem like terrorists. Not smart enough. But maybe they were hiding their intelligence. Nope, they were dopes. Whatever they were up to was probably just illegal and therefore highly profitable. I had learned that they were both as dangerous as scorpions when alarmed so I'd have to get inside the house when both were gone.

I watched the house like a hawk. I had to be on guard when the golden opportunity happened and both men left together. If it looked like they might be staying away a spell, I'd better be ready to go in.

I needed to get my crime kit ready to take along. It all had to fit into a small backpack so I'd have to choose my tools carefully.

What a joke. When I was done all I had was some dark clothes, pliers, a small flashlight, some nippers from the garden, and my perfect drawing of the house. Mary Jarvis, my best friend until we were ten and she moved away, lived next door in that house. I knew every crook and cranny. It might make old Derek nervous if he knew how much I knew. My crime kit sure wouldn't.

I almost cried when I thought of all the goodies I could be packing if my brother Mike wasn't so uptight about his police property. Goodies that would have made my job of ferreting out the evildoers a snap and kept me safe. Kevin gave me a nothing but a lot of holy lip about trusting God to see to the evil and being careful not to take a life for any reason. If I had listened to Father Kevin much longer, his life might have been the first to go.

Even Fitz was a selfish piglet. He could afford to hire some pros to back me. Pros with super equipment even the robbers or terrorists wouldn't have. I burned with the injustice of having three such useless big brothers.

I could have used a gun but I couldn't afford one and didn't like shooting anyway. Too noisy.

Ryan would be my backup. I could count on Ryan—responsible, rugged, and ready to serve, Ryan.

Finished with the pathetic packing of the crime kit, I got out the binoculars, went back to my spy spot on the living room couch and settled in. And just like that, Big Jim and Derek came out. Together. They were carrying lots of little Christmas wrapped packages. They were going to a Felon's Party, no doubt. The good boys looked busy. Surely they would be gone for an hour or so.

I called good old responsible Ryan and he didn't answer his phone. I called his folks' house and Mrs. Kelly said he had gone out.

"Not there? But where is he?" I said.

"He had to go to the store."

"But he doesn't even answer his phone."

"He can't," Mrs. Kelly laughed. "His phone didn't work. It needs batteries."

"Okay. I'll go by myself. I can do this. Just tell Ryan I forgive him and to meet me next-door to my folks ASAP. Tell him I'm going in now, alone."

"Amy, you're scaring me. You sound so dramatic. This isn't one of those ideas of yours that ends up on the front page is it? No one will get hurt, right? I don't want Ryan to get hurt. Or you either."

"Of course not, it's just a little game. Simple. Clean. Fun."

I didn't really think it would be any of those things but I got my mojo up and went next door. What I knew about the house, that those bozos didn't, came in darn handy. I knew that if you jiggled the lock on the study door that opens to a little patio in front, the door sometimes would pop open for you. After about twenty tries, it did. People never test the locks on homes they buy. The Jervis parents never knew about this little trick either, but all the kids did. Luckily, the not-so-nice boys didn't.

I was in and headed for the basement after turning off the heat. Luckily I knew where the thermostat was located. It was ten below zero in Minneapolis so it started to cool off quickly. It got colder as I headed down into the basement and darker and much, much damper. Actually it was more than damp. There was water on the walls and floor. The door into the main part of the basement was locked with a huge padlock. Then I remembered Mr. Jervis's tool room. I knew right where to look I hoped the sweet boys hadn't bothered with them.

They hadn't. I found a heavy prying tool and got back at the door. I couldn't budge it. They must have reinforced it or put on a new steel lined door. But they hadn't done anything with the plywood panels on either side. I took the crowbar to a panel and soon smashed a hole in it.

Avoiding as many splinters as I could, I slowly shinnied my way through the opening. It was hard. I was definitely giving up that malt before bed. My zaftig shape had started turning jumbo.

I stood up and gasped. There were no big pans cooking Meth. The room was filled with plants, row after row, all the way to the back of the big old amusement room. Tall, healthy looking plants with a shape and smell I thought I knew but would never admit knowing to my Dad. He thinks one puff will lead to harder drugs until I end up dead on the street.

Big Jim had said he was raising things for their garden but I doubted these plants were going in the back yard. They would be sold as prime, safe marijuana for enormous profit. And there were hundreds of plants. The dummies might have gotten rich. Except for me.

I walked around to check things out. Big Jim and Derek's organization was amazing. They had built cedar boxes for the rows of plants, each about two feet or more deep with nice rich soil inside. They had an automatic watering system that probably was timed to go on every hour or so with a soft mist. They also had a small gas furnace, which was on constantly with vents around the sides to keep all the plants at optimum temperature. There was a fancy computer that ran everything.

My plan was simple. I would destroy the whole system. I started by turning off the water. Then I turned off the burner and cut the cables when it cooled. They'd need some time to get that going. I erased all the programs on the computer and used my crowbar to smash it. In the meantime, the room was getting chilly but not cold enough yet to freeze. The plants wouldn't freeze in time. Too slow.

I needed a weed killer but I hadn't seen any in the tool room. I looked around for something else and had a great idea. Bleach! That kills anything you spray it on and it does it fast.

I headed to the laundry room and found a huge bottle of bleach and an empty spray bottle. I sprayed each plant and poured bleach around the roots. The plants were fading as fast as an Iowa football team facing the Minnesota Golden Gophers.

I was cold to the bone but I kept at it until every plant was dying. Time to flee. I shinnied back out the hole I'd made and tried to pull some pieces together so Derek and Jim might not notice right away what I'd done.

Then things went really bad. I almost had a heart attack when I heard the front door open and rough talking with lots of swearing. The boys were back and I was stuck in their basement. When they came down, they would kill me if they spotted me.

Think fast Amy! I'd hide until they got deep into the room and then make a break for the stairs. If I got up there fast enough, I could slam the door shut and I thought the door had a deadbolt that would lock them in.

I made for the little tool closet as soundlessly as possible. It was difficult to walk with cold, sloshing water under my shoes. But I got in and pulled the door almost shut.

The boys came roaring down the stairs swearing and arguing. They went right by my closet where I'd left the door a little ajar for a quick get-away.

Derek growled, "Jim, you frikkin moron. You forgot to turn on the heat. And it's even colder down here. Did you forget to pay the gas bill?"

"Don't give me any more shit, Derek or I might just shoot your teeth out. I forgot nothing. I ain't stupid. And I have a gun."

"You are stupid, Dumbo, but we ain't got time to argue. Let's check the plants."

I could hear them opening the lock on the big door.

Derek said, "Oh God, the plants are all dead."

Jim sounded ready to cry. "It wasn't me. I left things perfect. We've been had. That little bitch next door did this. She told me she knew I wasn't gay."

"Yah, stupido. You had to keep sniffing around her like a dog in heat. Now you can find her and kill her."

Jim laughed, "And what will we do with her dead body? They stink right away you know."

"We'll bury her with the dead plants."

"You can't get a broad in one of them tiny little boxes."

"She don't have to go in one box. We can cut her up and spread her around."

I can tell you I really didn't care for the sound of that. And my mother would never forgive me if she couldn't give me a decent funeral mass with rosary the night before. I had to get out of this while I had a chance. And Ryan should be here soon.

Big Jim said, "Sounds like a plan. But let's look at the back here first. Maybe some of them plants lived through it and we can save them."

They walked away planning my murder. I waited until their voices faded a bit and lit out for the stairs. I had a head start but it was close because my shoes were now waterlogged and I kept slipping and sliding. It made a lot of noise.

I clawed and crawled up those stairs with two maddened rats on my heels. I got to the top of the starts and shut the door but I wasn't fast enough to get it locked. I could hear the sound of breaking glass coming from the den. Ryan was on his way in. And the boys were almost out.

⸺⸺⸺⸺⸺⸺⸺⸺⸺⸺

Derek opened the door and it crashed into me, pinning me to the wall behind me. I could hear Ryan walk in and the sound of a gun as Derek shot him. I looked out to see my Ryan on the floor and I could see blood. I went crazy.

I crashed the door back against them and sent Derek wobbling. He was trying to kill me but he couldn't aim. I tackled him. I went in low, about at his knees and I butted him with my head with my whole body behind it. He teetered and got off a shot but it was high and wild. Then he fell straight back and into Big Jim three steps behind him and they both flew to the icy cement floor below. Both hit their heads with a noise that sounded like ripe melons smashing. And both lay there perfectly still. I locked the door and called 911 with one hand and felt Ryan for a pulse with the other. He was breathing but there was blood on his arm.

The police came and Ryan was taken to the hospital with me in the ambulance and everyone in both families following. He just had a flesh wound but he hit the floor when he fell and got kind of knocked out.

I got a lot of press in the papers for catching those "nice boys." Turns out they were wanted for murder in Indiana. This was their third drug bust, a mandatory life sentence in the U.S. Add that to murder and they would be in a federal prison forever. I got a Minneapolis Police Citizen Award, which drove my brothers nuts, and a money prize from the Crime Fighters.

It wasn't worth it though. There were only three people in both families who were still talking to me, Ryan, Bennett and Carter. Ryan because he's so nice and my little nephews because they live for exciting stuff and they think there's usually a little action where I am and that I'm quite crazy.

I think so too. I had almost killed my One, True Thing and my whole future when I put Ryan in front of that gun. I kept apologizing and promising him no more stupid investigations, never again.

But Ryan said, "Lovey, if I wanted a more traditional woman, I would have run like the wind when we first met. You were six and I was nine. You threatened to beat me up real good if I wouldn't admit that I loved you, in front of witnesses. You were adorable then and still are. Like the song says, I love you just the way you are."

That made me happier but I was determined to conquer my curiosity, rein in my ego and start acting like other women. I told everyone, "I am through with trouble and crime forever. No, really, I mean it. You could probably make book on that."

Ryan said, "And I'll bet Amy can find you a good bookie."

Joan Murphy Pride is an advertising writer in the Twin Cities. She feels the novel ways advertisements have with the truth have given her a terrific education in fiction writing. She loves a good mystery and hopes you like hers. Pride's first book *Not So Fast*, co-written with Phebe Hanson, was published by Nodin Press in 2006. It's available from Amazon.com and Barnes and Noble.com, and it's darn funny. Her second book, *Double-Cross Country,* is scheduled for release in 2011 by North Star Press.

A HOLLY JOLLY HOMICIDE

Dennis Anderson

THE TWIN CITIES OF MINNEAPOLIS and St. Paul are known for early, deep snowfalls. From the looks of the entryway, the snow the victim had tracked inside from the cold had long since melted, staining his oversized, fur-lined jacket. The dead man wore a bright red hat with a large white tassel, fur lined gloves and tall black, calfskin boots with genuine silver buckles. Wire-framed spectacles perched on the end of his nose magnified his round, plump cheeks which, despite an otherwise ashen complexion, still appeared rosy. Homicide Detective Mike Jergens crouched down next to the large, rotund body and was dead sure about two things. First, the man dressed as Santa Claus would not be making his appointed rounds on Christmas Eve. And second, if jolly 'ol St. Nick had been facing the North Pole when he was attacked, his clouded, lifeless eyes were gazing due south before his body hit the floor. Deep purple bruising visible above the fur collar of his red suit and the position of his head left no doubt that his neck had been snapped and violently twisted. One look was all it took to know. Someone had murdered Santa Claus.

MIKE JERGENS MOVED FROM THE MPD's Criminal Investigations to Homicide on a fast track. His intense, brooding presence at a crime scene was unnerving, even to department veterans. He rarely spoke during a homicide investigation, methodically scanning each room for anything that might seem out of place. That's no easy task when you're documenting evidence inside a crack house following a drug deal gone bad. This crime scene, however, was anything but typical.

If Mike was surprised to find a man dressed as Kris Kringle sprawled across the kitchen entry of a spotless, single-family home the week before Christmas, it didn't show on his face. His dispassionate approach to the job was well known to colleagues. As the crime scene technicians busied themselves documenting every aspect of the murder scene, Mike pawed through a pile of mail on the victim's dining room table. Santa's real name, it turned out, was James Earl Stevens. The utility bills for the one-and-a-half story home just south of Minnehaha Creek were up-to-date and there was a postcard reminding Santa to have his teeth cleaned. A huge stack of catalogs had arrived just in time for last minute holiday gift-giving. Detective Jergens also found several proxy notices and year-end reports from brokerage firms. Santa, it seemed, was well-invested in the markets.

There was a clatter at the back of the house as technicians processed the body and collected trace evidence, but otherwise the house was quiet, clean and cool. Santa Stevens kept his home an environmentally-friendly 68 degrees over the long winter nights. He also had exquisite taste or had the means to hire an interior decorator. The couch and armchair were genuine leather, floor length drapes swept back from the bay window, accentuating the coved ceiling and built-in Craftsman-style oak cabinets. The artwork, Mike noticed, were all original oils and charcoal sketches. Not one art store print in sight. And in most of the framed photographs scattered throughout the house, a large man with a white beard posed at landmarks around the world. Santa, by all appearances, enjoyed livin' large.

Before removing the body for a formal autopsy, the coroner's assistant at the scene verified what Mike had already guessed. Someone had twisted Jim Stevens head in a violent manner, breaking at least three of the vertebra in his neck in the process. There was no reason to believe the injuries were sustained in a fall. Time of death was estimated between ten and ten-thirty the previous night, which meant that Jim Stevens had been murdered approximately fifteen hours before his supervisor at the Prairie View Mall phoned the emergency contact telephone number in his file and just over sixteen hours before Jim's distraught brother had dialed 911.

An attractive, 30-something brunette wearing a sterile, white Tyvek jumpsuit, blue latex gloves and two digital cameras walked into the bedroom to find the lead investigator.

"Well, I guess I'm not getting that Barbie Prince and Princess Gift Set I asked for this year," MPD officer and crime scene photographer Maggie Summers said.

She hadn't necessarily expected Mike to laugh, but Maggie was annoyed when she got no response at all. Maggie was used to getting a response from the men in her life. She studied his face as he examined some papers on Jim Steven's bedside table.

"Helloooo? Detective?"

"Hmm? Sorry? Oh, Maggie!"

She was pleasantly surprised when Mike Jergens remembered her name from one crime scene to the next. Everyone knew he had an uncanny ability to block out distractions, but when he was on scene, colleagues often had to remind him to answer his own cell phone. As far as Maggie could tell, there didn't appear to be room in that man's head for anything of a personal nature, which might help to explain why a handsome, fit and intelligent man was still single at forty-two years old. He was a riddle all right, Maggie thought, but in her line of work solving puzzles was all in a day's work.

"I think I got everything I need, Mike, but thought I should check with you before I head back downtown. Can I do anything else for you?"

"No, thanks. Nice work, officer."

And that, apparently, was that. Maggie knew that when Mike Jergens said anything, it wasn't meant to be curt or dismissive, it was strictly business. And yet she couldn't shake a nagging feeling of disappointment or ease the knot in her stomach as she slowly turned to leave.

"Say, Maggie?"

And just like that, it was spring and Maggie felt butterflies. What was it about this aloof man that made her feel like she was seventeen again? She paused just long enough, she hoped, to add a bit of dramatic tension to their dialog.

"Yes, Mike?"

"How long before I can access crime scene photos?"

Photos? "I'll be sure to upload images to our local area network and email you a link just as soon as I get back to the office, *Detective.*"

"Okay, great. Thanks again, Maggie."

Men.

I DON'T REALLY GIVE A GOOD GODDAMN what your excuse is, little man, my daughter is here to see Santa's workshop." The irate mother was in a full-throated rant and would not be denied a full hearing. "I have to send photos of her sitting on Santa's lap to the grandparents in Florida. Which means I don't care if you have to dress up the Queen of England in a big red suit. Got it?!"

Peter Billings closed his eyes and took a slow, deep breath before answering. At just four-foot-six in his stocking feet and jingle-bell slippers, Pete was a natural to play Santa's Elf each Christmas. The kids were terrific. Lately, however, he could do without the aggressive and condescending behavior of the parents. Most made their fortunes downtown and their homes in the upscale neighborhoods and developments surrounding Prairie View Mall. Work was scarce this time of year, especially for a little person, so he bit his tongue and pasted a smile on his face before he said anything at all to the angry mom glaring down at him.

"Look, Ma'am, if you'd let me explain ..."

"Where is Santa Claus?" she hissed through clenched teeth.

Thankfully, before Pete lost both his temper and his job, a booming voice cut him off short.

"Peter Billings?"

A tall man wearing a dark suit and stern expression held a badge and ID at arms length as he approached, revealing a Smith & Wesson M&P45 in its shoulder harness as his jacket fell open. As if sensing a gathering winter storm, mother and child melted into the bustling throng of holiday shoppers like two ghosts of Christmas present.

"I'm Pete Billings. What can I do for you, officer?"

"My name is Jergens, Mr. Billings. I'm a detective with Minneapolis PD, looking into the circumstances surrounding the death of James Stevens. I found your name on Santa's list."

"Death? What are you talking about? I heard there was an accident."

"No, I'm sorry to say Mr. Steven's was murdered. How well did you know each other?"

Pete leaned back and reached for the red, braided rope that lined the path towards the massive display of brightly-painted plywood boxes which resembled a huge pile of Christmas gifts. The news of Jim's murder seemed to take him by surprise.

"Dead?! How did this happen?" Pete climbed on top of one the boxes next to Santa's velvet throne.

Mike ignored the question and asked one of his own.

"How well did you know the victim, Mr. Billings?"

"Well, you know, he was Santa Claus. Everyone tells me I look like an elf. I guess it was fate that we wound up working together. He's really *dead*?!"

"I found a list with your name on it at Mr. Steven's home," Mike said. "Any idea why?"

"Look, none of this is making sense. We're co-workers, that's all. I take the checks or process credit cards. Jim does the Ho-Ho-Ho's. Parents get a cute picture of their kids with Santa Claus. That's the deal." Pete shifted his weight on the box and looked Detective Jergens in the eye. "We went to Happy Hour after our shift at the mall one night, but that turned out to be a really, really bad idea. A little person and a fat man in a red suit draw quite a bit of attention in a room full of drunks. Let's just say the clever comments got real old, real fast and leave it at that."

"About Mr. Steven's list, it seems several names on it had been checked twice."

Pete grinned and said "It's like the song, Detective. Santa makes a list and checks it twice. Jim was a meticulous guy."

"When was the last time you saw Jim, Mr. Billings?"

"Well, it would have been the end of our shift last night," Pete said. "He seemed to be in a pretty good mood, but he was like that most of the time. Jim was always smiling."

"And then . . . ?"

"And he gave me a little wink before he dashed out of sight. He was late for a date, I think."

Mike wrote something in his notebook and looked up at Peter. "Nothing out of the ordinary, though? Anything you found unusual?"

"No. Well, he was wearing his costume when he left," Pete said. "I guess that's not all that unusual for Jim, but management doesn't like us walking around the mall in character. But you know Jim."

"I'm sorry, I never met the man."

"What I mean is Jim was Santa Claus 24/7. It wasn't enough for him to put on some weight and grow a beard. No. His suit was the real deal, too. Had it custom-tailored. See, being Santa was Jim's whole life."

"And you, Mr. Billings? What's your story?"

"Me? I'm an accountant. I do taxes, mostly. If I recall correctly, it was just over four years ago when Jim walked into my office with a sack full of receipts. He offered me the elf gig on the spot. "

"You said you were co-workers," Mike said.

"Sure. I did his taxes, too. See, once the Christmas season ends, tax season begins. When businesses mail their W2s at the end of the year, my accounting and financial planning business takes off. And I get to lose the jingle bells, curly-toed slippers and pointy foam ears."

Mike made another note. "Mr. Stevens did okay for himself working as a professional Santa?"

"Jim was set for life," the elf replied. "He worked for local advertising agencies, posing in ads for department stores and restaurants – that sort of thing. We did a television commercial together that went national, too. That was a bonanza. Round figures? Jim made a hundred thousand dollars each year."

"And is there good money playing Santa's Elf, Mr. Billings?"

"Not really. Residual checks are only sent to actors who have lines. Me? I got a day rate for filming. Jim was the actor. If you can call saying 'Ho Ho Ho' acting," Pete said.

"Can you think of anyone that had a problem with Mr. Stevens?" Mike continued, "Any enemies or difficulties on the job?"

"No. There were no jealous husbands this year that I know of, Detective."

Mike allowed his face to register a trace of emotion. He was honestly surprised. "Excuse me, *this* year? Was there trouble at the mall last year?"

"Talk about your bad Santa. Everybody knew Lauren was married," Pete said, "and her husband made sure Jim got the message loud and clear."

"Do you remember Lauren's last name?"

"Uh, no. I mean, maybe it's in the files at the mall office. But you know, nothing ever really came of it. You know how it goes. Everybody loves Santa."

"You mean Mr. Stevens?"

"That's what I said."

PARKER MCDONALD WAS A PRIGGISH, fifty six year old executive with Hansen Development Group. He'd spent the past four years as managing director of the Midwest division, running six properties from corporate offices inside the Prairie View Mall. Sprawling over several acres in a tony neighborhood west of the Twin Cities, residents in the surrounding countryside appreciated Prairie View's trendy shops and restaurants which catered to the nouveau riche.

"Yes, certainly, I remember quite well, Detective. Thankfully, we were able to keep it a private matter."

"Was this the first incident involving Santa? That is to say, Mr. Stevens?"

"The one and only, Detective. Mr. Stevens' liaison with Mrs. Lauren Grant and the subsequent visit to our mall by Mr. Grant was the only black mark in his personnel file. It seems Mrs. Grant had what Mr. Grant called a 'Santa complex', sexually aroused by the costume, or the character, or both," Parker McDonald said with flat affect. "Mr. Grant, who has had to endure this yearly embarrassment, confided in me that some women never get over their fascination with Santa. He's the one man, you see, permitted midnight visits."

"Just to clarify, Mr. Grant spoke freely with you about his wife's proclivities?"

"Sadly, her infidelities with other seasonal employees had become commonplace in their marriage. Naturally, we at Prairie View Mall discourage relationships with our guests, but we had never before received even a whisper of impropriety regarding Mr. Stevens. There were none following this unfortunate event. Everyone loved Mr. Stevens."

"This was, however, a professional embarrassment for you," Mike said. It wasn't a question. It bordered on an accusation.

"Quite. And while I may have harbored suspicions Jim was, shall we say, spreading holiday joy where it would be inappropriate, I also believe he valued his association with us. He was quite talented in the role and was paid a king's ransom for his duties."

"Perhaps you could help me with a few names on Santa's list, Mr. ..."

"Parker, please," McDonald said.

"Parker, who did Mr. Stevens know with the initials C.B.?"

"Candice. I mean to say, Ms. Bahr. She works in seasonal sales and mall merchandising. You'll find her either at our Christmas kiosk in front of Macy's, or helping out in the central court. I've had great difficulty keeping her out of Santa's Workshop of late. I know she was very fond of Jim."

EVEN WITH PUFFY, TEAR-FILLED EYES and a runny red nose, Candice Bahr was one fabulously good-looking elf.

"Lauren was a real horse's fanny – but her husband was even worse."

Candice blew her nose and wiped a dark trail of mascara down the side of her face. The young woman referred to on the victim's Christmas list was an attractive, twenty-something blond with more than one tattoo peeking out from beneath her skintight green jumper and red tights. It appeared as though she'd tried to color-coordinate the small emerald stone in her left nostril, but Mike left that detail out of his report. He did, however, allow himself to wonder whether Santa's Workshop attracted more dads than moms when Candice was working the rope-line.

When she wasn't working with Peter Billings at Santa's Workshop, Candice split her time between leading aerobics classes at Lifetime Fitness and sitting next to a five by seven foot booth with a red canvas awning. She sold everything from coffee mugs and stuffed animals, to Christmas tree ornaments and cigarette lighters. The awning and gifts all bore the slogan: **PRAIRIE VIEW MALL: the mall for y'all.** Mike held an ornament at arms length and furrowed his brow.

"I know, right? See, they own a mall in Atlanta, too. Can you believe it?" Although she wasn't chewing bubblegum at the moment, Mike imagined he could hear it each time she opened her mouth.

"You were saying that after Jim's affair with Mrs. Grant, Mr. Grant showed up at Santa's Workshop. Mr. McDonald did not include your statements in his report, otherwise, it's quite detailed. What can you tell me about the fight, Ms. Bahr?"

"Candy, everyone calls me Candy."

"About Lauren's husband?"

"Right. So, he walks right past the line of kids, right up to Santa, looked him right in the eye and called him a stocking stuffer. You know, a mother stuffer. Well, it was something like that."

"And when you say Santa, you mean . . . ?"

"Jim, silly! Everybody called Jim Santa."

"Ms. Bahr, it's important that you tell me *exactly* what was said."

"Oooo, no, that would be naughty. Santa says good girls," and with that she stopped talking. From all appearances, Candice stopped breathing as well. Her narrow shoulders shook as she wept and several minutes passed before Candy found her voice again.

"You can tell me, Candy. Mr. Stevens would want you to be honest."

"Ah, shit, alright, I admit it. I loved the big jerk. Santa – was – my – boyfriend."

BACK AT CITY HALL, ARMED WITH several more names Candy had helped I.D. from the list, Mike worked the phones and conducted several interviews.

"Mr. Grant? My name is Jergens, I'm with the Minneapolis Police Department. Yessir. I need you to come down for an interview about an altercation you had with a local actor who played Santa Claus. No, sir, this would have been last year. Yessir, at Prairie View Mall. I see. Well then, this would be a *different* Santa Claus, wouldn't it, sir? I'll need you to come to my office, Room 108, City Hall?Anytime between two and five. Uh huh, fine, we'll see you then, sir. And Merry Christmas."

MOST OF THE NAMES ON SANTA'S LIST WERE those you'd expect to find. Mike had identified a dozen co-workers, several relatives and Jim Steven's dental hygienist (who was, as it turned out, a size two, preferred black, and shopped at Victoria's Secret). He wondered about the personal nature of the gift and remembered the postcard from a dentist he found on the victim's dining room table. Perhaps Ms. 'size two' has a husband or a boyfriend.

Santa had definitely been a very, very naughty boy. The personal items listed next to Candy Bahr's initials (in size one), suggested to Mike that murderous jealousy might come in all sizes. He made a note to discuss Santa's injuries with the medical examiner and determine the amount of force required to twist and break a man's neck in that manner. Candy was small, but potentially very strong.

Jim Stevens, a.k.a. Santa, had purchased friends and co-workers fruit baskets, sweaters, hats and gloves. Pete Billings was down for a bottle of wine. No big deal. No real clues, either. And once again as his mind spun out theories, connections and motives, Detective Jergens was oblivious to anything else in the room. Phones rang. Files drawers slammed shut. And although Mike didn't notice, as every other man in the room did, Maggie Summers worked every inch of the faded linoleum like a catwalk in her after-work heels and designer jeans. The sharp report of her heels stopped just behind his chair and Maggie's Private Collection Jasmine White Moss perfume failed to penetrate his ruminations. She peeked over his shoulder at Santa's list of unmentionables and sex toys and breathed into his ear.

"Oh my God. Are you moonlighting in Sex Crimes again?"

That sent Jim to bolt upright. He turned to find Maggie's bright, mischievous smile taunting him. The jeans and layered shirt combo was a marked improvement over the sterile jumpsuits she wore to crime scenes. She turned her body and leaned a hip against the desk.

"That's quite a list, Detective. Shopping for anyone I know?"

"What? No! Look Maggie – it's not my list, thank you very much. It belongs to the victim."

"Looks like Santa's been a naughty boy."

"She's in amazing shape and you know," Mike said, "she's really kind of attractive. For an elf."

"She? Well whoever she is, she's getting more toys from Santa than anyone else on the list."

"There's something about this girl. The ears are a bit odd, but the costume ..." Mike said, drifting off in thought.

"Alright, Mike! I get it." Maggie gave him a playful punch on the shoulder and regretted it immediately. *What am I, in third grade?*, she thought to herself.

Mike didn't seem to notice. He was still focused on the motives the list suggested. "This is only a partial list of Santa's helpers. Five other names have something personal marked for delivery to their stockings. And from the in-terviews so far, his 'ghosts of Christmas past' were pretty friendly, too."

Mike's phone blinked. He reached to answer it before Maggie could reply.

"Mike Jergens. Yes? Could you escort him to Interview One? Thanks."

He swiveled in his chair to face Maggie and found his face was now inches from her hers. She had turned and placed her palms on the desk and was leaning in to study the 'personal' items a bit closer. Mike's face betrayed nothing, even when his highly trained detective skills noted, with interest, Maggie's blouse had fallen open and her curly brown hair framed her profile perfectly.

"Jealous husband in for questioning," Mike said.

"The wife getting personal with Santa?"

"Not *this* year." Mike pushed his chair back away from the desk and stood up to leave. "Evidently it was very personal a year ago. There's a pattern here."

"Where you find one jealous husband . . . " Maggie began.

"I expect to find others," Mike concluded.

"Mike, before you go, did you look at the photos from the scene?"

"Yes. Yes, I did. One thing stood out."

"Let me guess," Maggie said. "The storage bench by the backdoor?"

Mike smiled and collected his notes.

"You'll make Detective any day now, Maggie."

· ·

J̲UST HOW MANY SANTAS ARE WE talking about, Mr. Grant?"

"Listen, this may seem like a big joke to you, but it's recurring issue in my marriage. Trust me, I've tried everything. Lauren is a nightmare before Christmas."

"I apologize, Mr. Grant. Why don't we focus on the incident at Prairie View?"

"I knew she up to her old tricks again. I found three sets of pictures of our kids with the same Santa. So I took a day off work and followed her to the mall. I admit it. I went right up to the asshole and gave him a piece of my mind. Look, I'm not proud of what I said in front of the kids. But there was no way some asshole like that was going to keep seeing my wife and my kids. No way."

"So, the two of you fought?"

"I wouldn't call it a fight," Mr. Grant said, "but I'd have stuffed him inside his own bag of gifts if he didn't have a little girl sitting in his lap. Then the elf gets into it."

Mike made a note and asked "So, Santa had a helper?"

"That's what I said. An elf. Short guy, pointy ears? He wraps himself around my leg, trying to pull me away," Mr. Grant said. "He was out of control."

"There was no mention of any of this in the mall files," Mike said.

"I could have sued the girl, too. See this?" Mr. Grant turned and pointed at the side of his face. "You can still the marks where that little bitch scratched my face."

Mike allowed his stoic façade to crumble and looked genuinely puzzled.

"The little girl scratched you?"

"No, no, the other elf. The babe. Man was she hot, in more ways than one. A real looker. And she slapped him good, too."

"The elf," Mike said.

"No." Mr. Grant was clearly growing exasperated. "Santa Claus."

"Let's start over. How many helpers did Santa have during your altercation?"

"Two. First the little guy, then the stunner."

"A young woman? Can you describe her for me, please?"

"Pretty, thin, she had tattoos. She was really built, too, did I mention that? Had a green dress on that looked like a second skin," Mr. Grant explained. "Her belly button? An 'innie,' guaranteed."

"I get the picture. So tell me what happened next."

"Well, the girl lit into the Santa but good. He's throwing up his hands and trying to get away."

"How would you describe her emotions?"

"Jealous," Mr. Grant said, smiling now. "Crazy jealous. She went wild. Santa was in big trouble with that girl."

"And the little person?"

Mr. Grant stared at the table for a moment, thinking. "He surprised me. I turned around and was looking him right in the eye. He was on top of the gift boxes, pointing his stubby finger at me and and telling me I wasn't welcome, he's reporting me to security, how would I like it if he came to my office and chased away business. Like that."

"And that was it?" Mike asked, "You never went back?"

"Look. I had nothing to do with whatever, okay? This is old news, Detective. Just ask me for my alibi and let me get on my merry way, okay?"

"Are you in some kind of hurry, Mr. Grant?"

"It's the week before Christmas, Detective. Have you not been paying attention?"

* * *

Mike was fairly certain that he had eliminated one suspect, but felt Santa's list might still yield a suburban dad with an axe to grind. In the meanwhile, he would follow another possible motive for murder. If not for love, it could be the money.

Enter the accountant from the city's budget office, a small, ferret-faced man named Howard Bean. He was both short and thin and Mike wondered whether Mr. Bean would cast a shadow in the noonday sun. His brown suit looked well worn and his cheap shoes were scuffed. He was, by all appearances, a frugal man.

"I believe eighty thousand dollars or more is missing," he squeaked.

"And that's based on what, exactly?"

It was clear that money could prove to be as strong a motive for murder as Jim's affairs.

"My preliminary review of Mr. Steven's last five tax returns and current holdings. What I can't find at the moment," Mr. Bean recounted, "are statements from several accounts that seem to be posted from a different mailing address. I've found automatic debits on five revolving lines of credit pulling funds from two different accounts. It looks like close to five thousand dollars a month on each, going back for quite some time. He must have known that the money was going out."

"Unless someone was intercepting the mail," Mike said.

"Maybe. But I don't have current records on those accounts," Mr. Bean explained. "I have routing numbers and amounts, but without a court order I can't give you a name."

"So, you're telling me I'm looking for someone who understands money."

"I didn't say that," Mr. Bean said. "For all we know, Mr. Stevens could have been supporting someone. All I know is that two of his accounts were bleeding money. One account showed no activity until the beginning of last year. Steady withdrawals ever since."

"So let's say he's paying someone's bills," Mike said, "financing their good life. And then, what? He adds another girlfriend?"

"I can't say. We could be looking at recurring payments on a credit balance, a savings account direct-deposit, or he was funneling money into a brokerage account to purchase mutual funds. It could be anything. All I have so far is a list of account numbers and financial institutions. It will take awhile to get a court order and unravel it all."

Mike made several more notes on his pad. "I have a couple threads I can tug on to get some answers right away. Thanks for your help."

· ·

I WANT TO THANK BOTH OF YOU FOR COMING IN," Mike began, "I've got some questions about Jim Stevens that I believe the two people who knew him best can answer for me."

Candy watched her reflection in the mirrored glass, shifting in her seat now and then to tug the knit fabric of her jumper over her shapely, toned thighs or pick imaginary lint off her chest. Though a natural extrovert, Candy now found herself feeling exposed by the close quarters in the interview room. Peter sat on the edge of the conference table with his feet on the chair, arms crossed defiantly across his chest. Peter's body language was easy to read. His crossed arms were a subconscious desire to place a wall between himself and the official questioning.

"So tell me, Candy, what was Parker McDonald's reaction when he learned Santa Jim was delivering more than gifts to the condominium he purchased for you in Excelsior?"

Candy was startled. "I beg your pardon?"

It was clear that although she was wearing quite a bit of makeup, the accusation of an affair with the very staid manager at Prairie View Mall made Candy blush.

Mike continued, "Two years ago, just after you started working at the mall, Parker McDonald took control of a fully furnished showroom condominium at one of the properties he managed. The Prairie Overlook Development?"

Candy blinked, squirmed and straightened her skirt.

"As managing partner of the Midwest division, Parker leased the unit, at cost, in your name, but made the payments from an account in his name only. You do live at Number Two, Prairie Overlook Drive in Excelsior, correct?"

"Well, sure, Mr. McDonald helped me find a place. I was new in town."

"Mr. McDonald lives on the lake in Wayzata with his wife, correct?"

"Parker was very nice to me when I first moved into the city, Detective."

"And was Mr. McDonald still 'very nice' following your jealous altercation with Jim Stevens at Santa's Workshop? By all accounts, you were furious with Jim for sleeping with Lauren Grant. Did Mr. McDonald ask you if Santa was sneaking down the chimney at Overlook Drive?"

Candy didn't seem to have an answer, but her eyes grew moist and she began to blink rapidly.

"Let me just work through my notes," Mike said, "and you two jump in if you think I get something wrong, okay? I know Candy set up a credit card for herself on Jim's dime. I'm guessing you spent most of your time at Jim's hoping to intercept 'letters to Santa' from the credit card company."

Candy chewed at her lower lip and pouted. Her full, moist lips glistened. Without moving her head, her large, pale blue eyes found Mike's and held his gaze. Mike was convinced this look had served Candy well in the past.

"You're the tax expert, Pete," Mike said, turning his attention to the little man at the end of the table. "How did you explain those missing funds to the IRS? You prepared his tax returns."

Pete shifted his weight, scowled and remained silent.

"Okay Pete, try this. Tell me what Candy said when you confronted her with your suspicions. Since it's clear you had to be involved in the cover up, can you tell me what Candy did to convince you to keep quiet?"

"I'm not sure I like what you're insinuating, Detective," Pete said.

"I believe Candy used all of her considerable charms to convince you to keep your mouth shut," Mike said. "I believe that, living out your centerfold fantasy with Candy was more than you ever dreamed possible for yourself, Pete."

"Candy loves me!"

Although that was clearly her cue, Candy sat mute and stared at the table.

"How many different phantom companies did Santa invest in last year, Pete? How did it feel when you learned Jim had retained the services of your competitor, Cooper Asset Management in St. Paul? What was the plan after you were served with a request to produce all federal and state returns going back five years, Pete?"

Candy and Pete exchanged a glance but neither one said a word.

"Did Candy give you her key to Jim's place," Mike said, "or did you have a copy made while he was working? And why is it you're always climbing on the furniture?"

Pete frowned and Candy blushed. Both watched closely as Mike opened a manila folder and slowly and deliberately placed eight by ten color enlargements of the crime scene on the desk between them. The first photo showed the back entryway to Jim's house. Next was Jim Stevens in his Santa costume laying dead in the tiled entry by the back door. Mike laid a photo on the table showing the body and the six foot long bench with hinged cover where Santa stored winter boots and hats and mittens. And finally, a brightly lit, Kodak color close-up of two small, boot-shaped puddles of melted snow on top of the storage box.

"There was only one way for you to get the upper hand with someone Jim's size, Pete. I think you needed to climb up on the bench to get the leverage required to snap his neck. Jim probably didn't even see you, hidden from sight by the door as he entered the house. But when he closed the door, he found himself face to face with a killer."

Peter Billings didn't move. He didn't even twitch.

"Didn't your mom tell you not to climb on the furniture, Pete? I guess you never outgrew it."

Candy started crying in earnest, her breath coming in ragged gasps.

"I didn't know he was going to kill Santa. Honest. I just needed the money!"

"Shut up you stupid whore," Pete said.

"My goodness, you're an angry elf," Mike said. "And you have such a short temper."

* * *

So it seems clear that Candy was sleeping with McDonald, Santa Claus and the Elf."

"Do you think she knew Pete planned to kill Santa Claus?" Maggie looked stunning with her curly hair pulled back and knotted carefully.

She had poured herself into a little black dress and matching heels for the party gearing up in the squad room.

"Well, the two of them have stopped talking. The exam of Jim's financial records gave us more than enough evidence to charge both with grand theft. It's up to the lawyers now whether one or both are charged on the murder. They want results from the state lab in St. Paul," Mike said. "But you know, finding her DNA at the scene won't prove much, given her history."

The voices in the room grew louder after one of the detectives turned up the volume on a portable CD stereo playing "Jingle Bell Rock".

"Are you going to stay for the Christmas party, Mike? It's Christmas Eve, you know."

"Actually, I might run over over to HCMC. I need a copy of the autopsy results on Santa Claus from the Hennepin County Medical Examiner before I can file this one away."

"HO HO HO! Merry Christmas!"

Mike and Maggie turned to see a ratty-looking, synthetic beard-wearing colleague in a lumpy red suit walk into the squad room. By anyone's standards, Lt. Dishman wasn't even close to being a convincing Kris Kringle, but he seemed to enjoy himself.

"Don't go. It's time for the 'Secret Santa' gift exchange," Maggie said. "Who'd you pick, Mike?"

"HO, HO, HO! Santa's got something in his bag for you, Maggie," Lt. Dishman bellowed. "Have you been a good girl this year?"

"Randy, I'm *always* good."

"Maggie, you'd make a good dog want to break his chain. HO, HO, HO!"

Maggie ripped brightly colored paper off her large present and stared in disbelief at the gift her 'Secret Santa' had chosen. It was her very own Barbie Prince and Princess Gift Set.

"I know he had flaws," Mike said, "but I still think every girl should believe in Santa Claus."

Dennis Anderson is a local Twin Cities' writer who has spent the past thirty years writing for both print and broadcast media across the upper Midwest. Dennis wrote, designed and published "Minnesota Country" for K102-FM. Affectionately known as "WordMan" to colleagues (a nickname he's been unable to shake for nearly 15 years), he is an accomplished broadcast copywriter, earning both the Galaxy and RadioBest awards for his efforts. Dennis makes his home in New Hope, MN with his wife, Stephanie and sons Bennett and Carter.

INSIDE THE GINGERBREAD HOUSE

Kathleen Lindstrom

I WAS THE ONE WHO FOUND HER BODY.

She was lying in the backseat of my car, a rented dark blue Taurus, four-door, the last one on the lot, the one I was "damn lucky to get"—or so the crabby Enterprise clerk told me, it being the week before Christmas and all.

And there she was.

At first, I thought she was sleeping. She was on her back, knees up, one arm hanging off the seat, the other placed on her left breast, as if pledging allegiance to the flag. Her mouth was slightly open, her eyes shut. But she was wearing short-sleeved cotton pajamas—which was the next clue something was wrong. It was freezing, even in that attached garage.

I searched for a pulse and felt how cold she was. That's when I covered my mouth so I wouldn't scream.

I brushed hair off her face and curled it back behind her ear, the way she liked it. I patted her hand. I told her everything would be okay and realized how ridiculous it sounded. I started to cry.

Then I saw a brown tassel on the floor mat that hadn't been there before. I snatched it up and put it in my pocket. I shouldn't have. But I did. I still don't know why.

I thought about everything for awhile, before running back into the kitchen to call nine-one-one. Then I sat and waited. And soon after, the truth inside that house cracked open like a rotten egg, oozing lies and betrayal all over the place.

But maybe I should start from the beginning.

I HAD ARRIVED IN MINNESOTA TWO DAYS EARLIER. The minute I got off the plane, I remembered why I had left this state in the first place.

It was ten below zero. The wind chill was forty-something below. It had also snowed the day before—eighteen inches, the radio weather guy kept bragging. And to top it off, the wind was blowing snow everywhere, which created something called a white-out, which means you can't see where the road ends and the sky begins—or whether you're heading into a ditch or a snow drift. It's like driving inside a white balloon.

But conditions improved when I reached the city. The main streets were plowed and open to traffic—which was moving like sludge anyway, thanks to the blizzard-like wind. Despite these hazards, people were on the road—visiting relatives for the holidays, probably, or heading downtown for some last-minute shopping.

I'm an idiot. What am I doing here?

"Addie, you have to come."

That was our conversation a few weeks earlier when Caroline called and asked me to spend Christmas with her and Doyle, and a few other friends who had no place to go during the holidays.

"It'll be fun," she said.

"It's too expensive, I can't afford it."

"Just the airfare. You'll stay with us. You'll eat here. You won't need money for anything else."

"A car rental. I'll need a car."

"We'll pick you up at the airport and take you back."

I stalled, realizing I would never rely on someone else for transportation, knowing I might need a quick getaway, not knowing how to explain that without sounding weird.

"Addie?" she asked.

"Mmmm?"

"It would be so good to see you again."

"Yeah."

The temperature was 60-something when we had this conversation. I was curled up on a couch in my studio apartment in Carmel, California, which sits over a bakery and smells like raisin bread, fudge brownies, coconut macaroons, breads, or chocolate chip cookies, depending on the day of the week. I had just returned from walking Olivia, my dog, who was sleeping in a puddle of sunshine under the window, exhausted from her afternoon romp along the ocean.

And then, out of the blue, Caroline said: "Addie, something strange is going on."

It turned out she'd been getting threatening letters in the mail—the kind with words cut from magazines and newspapers and pasted down, one by one, on a sheet of paper.

"Isn't that spooky?" she asked.

"No kidding! Especially with all the technology nowadays. Who'd go to all that trouble? What do they say?"

"They're just odd. They scare me. I'll show them to you when you get here."

"Have you called the police or anything?"

"No . . . I can't. Will you come? Please? You're the only one I can talk to."

I have a hard time saying no to people who beg, and I hadn't been back home for years; so I said yes and soon wished I hadn't. I had forgotten how painful below zero weather can be (a million tiny needles piercing your face) and how slippery conditions can send you into places you don't want to go.

<hr>

Eventually, I found Summit Avenue in St. Paul, a once-elite neighborhood overlooking the city. It was originally settled by railroad and lumber barons in the nineteenth century, men who'd built bigger and grander mansions just to outdo each other. They're dead, of course, but their homes endure—like aging divas, still stately and proud, but with peeling paint and sagging foundations.

Caroline and Doyle bought one of these crumbling Victorians a few years back and restored it to its original turn-of-the-century luster—all three floors, six bedrooms and five baths of it. Some local magazine featured it in their special *Homes with a History* edition, which embarrassed Caroline, but delighted Doyle, who likes the limelight.

Caroline is the evening news anchor for Channel 12. Doyle is an attorney at a big law firm, known for keeping the bad guys out of jail.She'd tell you about their perfect life and perfect house, but only if you asked her, and then she'd quickly change the subject to talk about *you*.

It was part of her charm.

I finally arrived at their house, which sat at the far end of a large lot buried in snow. It had tall thin windows and a round tower with a roof resembling a witch's hat. The front porch had lacy posts and spindles and wrapped around one side of the building. Actually, it looked like a gingerbread house—with lots of different shapes piled up and cobbled together in unexpected ways.

I parked at the end of the driveway, grabbed my suitcase from the back seat, lugged it up the porch steps and rang the bell, which *ding-donged* twice. Caroline's face appeared behind a beveled window, distorting her perfect smile.

"Addie! You made it. Come in. I'm so glad you're here."

She was as pretty as I remembered, a bit tired looking, but still beautiful: petite, blond hair, blue eyes, peaches and cream complexion, dimples, pouty lips, perfect teeth, perfect smile, perfect everything. I was ready to hate her the minute I met her in our freshman dorm, realizing I'd be rooming with Heather Locklear. But hating Caroline is impossible. Instead, we became good friends. She was as humble and sweet as she was beautiful and smart.

We hugged and chatted about the weather, the trip, the drive, the traffic, the hassles of air travel, and the fact that neither of us looked a day older, which made us laugh. The foyer was bigger than my living room and kitchenette combined. Garlands of evergreen and red ribbon wound around the room and up the grand staircase. The smell of pine and apple cider filled the house.

I thought about my plastic tree back home that smelled like mildew and dust.

Caroline led me to up my room—a surprisingly modern bedroom decorated in blues and whites, with four windows letting in the afternoon light. I felt better immediately. Best of all, l had my own bathroom.

"This is beautiful," I told her. "Nicer than any hotel."

"I'll let you unwind a bit," she said. "We'll eat about six. The dining room is easy to find; just follow your nose. We have a good cook. Two other people will be joining us."

She had a cook. I had a broken microwave.

Just then, a man stuck his head in the door—late thirties, very tall, athletic looking, salt and pepper hair, needing a haircut, maybe a shave, a bit stooped, a wry smile. Something purred inside and I found myself perking up.

"You made it." He was making a statement.

"About twenty minutes ago," I told him. "And about eighty degrees ago."

He looked confused, but entered the room anyway to shake my hand. "I'm Mark Royston, a friend of Doyle's."

"And this is my friend Addie," Caroline announced. "Addison Monroe. She just flew in from California. We went to St. Cloud together. She's a well known painter." Caroline was in her anchor mode now. "She sells a lot of her works along the Pacific coast."

"Well, but I . . . "

Caroline wouldn't let me finish. Actually, I'd only sold six paintings in ten years; and was working on a new commission, which might pay January's rent.

"She's very modest," Caroline went on. "She'll be famous some day."

This seemed to interest Mark, and he joined Caroline in beaming back at me, waiting for some kind of response.

"Well it beats hooking," I blurted out, "but not by much."

Fortunately, they chuckled and then excused themselves. "I'll let you rest and freshen up a bit," Caroline said. "See you at six."

I watched Mark walk down the hall to his room three doors away. He was wearing a blue sweater and tight jeans that showed off his cute little butt.

Hmm...

I NAPPED LONGER THAN I INTENDED and was late for dinner.

And Caroline was right. All I had to do to was follow my nose. The smell of tomato sauce lured me into a big dining room, where pastas, salads and breads were piled on a large table, reminding me how hungry I was.

Mark, Caroline and another man were already seated and too busy filling their faces to notice me. Doyle was walking around the table pouring wine, talking and laughing, trying to get the party going.

"There she is!" he boomed when he saw me. He wrapped me in a bear hug—all five-foot-seven, 150 pounds of him. I hadn't seen Doyle since their wedding reception and forgot how small he was—but how good looking: thick black hair, blue eyes, long lashes, blinding-white teeth, sexy smile. His effusive greeting surprised me, because we barely knew each other.

He pulled out my chair, got me settled and then introduced me to Mark, whom I'd already met, and whose eyes, I noticed for the first time, were hazel. Or green? Maybe light brown. He winked, which set off that purr phenomenon again. Then I met Orin, a large, meaty man whose muscles were turning to fat. Then a young woman dressed in jeans and a UM sweat shirt, standing apart from the group.

"And this is Anya," Doyle announced, "the miracle worker who cooks these amazing meals for us and makes our lives so easy by keeping us on track and cleaning up our messes."

Anya was in her early twenties. She had a school girl's body, brown hair in a ponytail, pale skin, and smudges under two fierce eyes that seemed to find me and pin me down like a specimen in her bug collection. I nodded at her, anyway, and tried to smile. She nodded back (no sign of a smile), then slipped into the kitchen.

"Anya's an interesting story," Doyle tried to explain. "She and her father fled Russia and he was charged with murdering his business partner here in St. Paul. I was on the defense team, but we lost and he was sentenced to life. They were going to send Anya back to Russia and she was terrified. Begged me to help. So we gave her a job and a place to stay. She cooked and cleaned for her father. Now she's cooking and cleaning for us, for . . . what? . . . " He turned to Caroline for confirmation. "Almost four years now?"

Caroline was busy stabbing at a cherry tomato in her salad, looking frustrated because it wouldn't cooperate. Or maybe angry. I couldn't tell.

"Yeah," she mumbled. "About that."

Then Orin piped in. "Now tell her the real story. How her father was escaping life in the Russian mafia. How he killed his partner by cutting off his head—leaving it in a trash can in Minnehaha Park. Calling it an honor killing."

"Yeah, well they're a different breed. What can I say?"

"You can say when we'll be leaving for Afton Alps tomorrow morning," Mark said, changing the subject. "And why in the world I'd want to go skiing in Minnesota when I grew up in Burlington, Vermont, the ski capital of the world."

"Ski capital, my ass," Doyle laughed. "Isn't it one of the top cities for senior citizens? Didn't AARP write something about that?"

Their banter lightened the mood and helped me relax, so I could sit back, focus on my food, listen to the conversation and get to know everyone a little better.

I learned the men would be spending the next day, Christmas Eve, skiing at Afton Alps. It was east of the city and had a lot of hills to choose from, according to Doyle, including several bunny hills in case Mark got scared on the *big-boy* hills.

Mark then told us about when he was interning at Hennepin County Medical Center, and Doyle had screamed like a girl. Mark, I learned, was a pediatrician in Boulder. He and two friends snuck young, "hot-shit-lawyer" Doyle into the morgue to show him what a dead body looked like. The dead body, however, shot up from under the sheet, which elicited a piercing screech from Doyle.

"You peed in your pants," Mark laughed.

"Never happened," Doyle retorted. "This story gets more colorful every time you tell it."

Caroline then announced "us girls" would go shopping while "you guys" were breaking legs on the slopes and told Doyle to leave out plenty of money—which elicited groans, *pretending*, of course, because Caroline had plenty of her own money to spend.

"See what you missed?" Doyle said to Orin. "You could be in the poor house now, just like me."

That's when I learned Orin and Caroline had been high school sweethearts, broke up in senior year, hooked up again after college, got engaged and planned to marry—until she met Orin's friend Doyle who swept her away to Las Vegas for a quickie wedding.

"Broke my heart," said Orin. "I'll never love again."

"Don't let him kid you," Mark assured me. "He's had more girl-friends than George Clooney."

"We knew we were wrong for each other," said Caroline. "We fought like cats and dogs."

"Yeah, but making up was *sooo* much fun."

"We would have killed each other if we'd gotten married."

"Yeah," Orin said. "I think you're right."

Suddenly, Anya was with us, floating into the room like a feather, unnoticeable until she started clearing food from the table. How long had she been there? Then I saw something odd—or thought I did: Anya standing behind Doyle, bending over to remove his plate, her hand brushing his hand, her hand lingering, him letting it linger, him not moving, his face frozen, hers in a smile.

Could it be?

Then Anya straightened up, balancing plates and saucers in both hands, all business now. "Dessert anyone?"

On CHRISTMAS EVE MORNING, Caroline showed me the letters.

We were sitting in the dining room, where Anya had filled the buffet with a huge continental breakfast—croissants, muffins, bagels, cereals, juices, fruits, scrambled eggs, sausages, marmalades, jams, cheeses, teas—enough food for a family of fifty. I grabbed a mug and headed for the coffee pot, needing to jumpstart my brain. I was still operating on Pacific time and felt hung over from last night's wine. Plus, I am not a nice person until I get my morning coffee.

The guys had left for their ski trip an hour or so earlier, which is what woke me up in the first place. All that clatter and those loud voices made me even crankier than usual.

Caroline, who was a morning person, sat across from me, cradling that old marble-blue coffee mug she'd had since college, jabbering away: "How was your sleep?" "How'd you like Mark?" "How's Hank?" "What did you think of Orin?" "When do you want to go shopping?""Are you okay?" "Are you mad at me?" "You look angry."

Eventually, she remembered what I'm like in the morning and decided to get out of there, grabbing a huge, carmel-dripping cinnamon roll on the way, which made me remember how Caroline could out-eat most men and never gain a pound.

Bitch.

She returned about forty minutes later, after I had finished five cups of coffee and a plate of eggs, sausages and raisin toast slathered with peanut butter and jelly. She figured I was de-fanged by then, and brought me those letters.

"Are you okay? Is the real Addison back among the living?"

I laughed. "I think so. Pea soup isn't spewing out of my mouth, is it?"

"No pea soup. No head spinning in circles."

"Oh, good." I smiled back. "Can we start all over again?"

She chuckled. Then she reached over to squeeze my hand, her eyes glistening now, her expression serious. "I'm so glad you're here. You don't know how much."

How can you not come running to help someone like this?

"Here are the letters I talked about. Look at them. Tell me what you think."

They were in envelopes, each postmarked from the main post office. The cut-out words were pasted down on cheap twenty-pound paper. Four had arrived since September; each dated the first of the month.

The first one read:"You won't get away with it we want justice"

The next one: "He didn't have to die. When will you tell the truth"

The next: "Seventeen years ago today. Time is running outIt's up to you"

The final letter, sent in December, was the most threatening: "You had your chance. More than you gave him. Are you ready to die"

"Carrie, my God! This is awful! Have you told anyone? Have you notified the police?"

"I can't."

"What do you mean you can't! You have to."

"But I can't."

"I don't understand. What's going on?"

She covered her face with her hands and shook her head, trying to find words. I waited. Suddenly, she looked ten years older.

Finally, "Do you remember our junior year at St. Cloud? We went to that Halloween party at some guy's house?"

It was seventeen years ago. We went to a lot of parties back then. "No, I don't remember."

"You went as Cher. Me as a gypsy?"

"Vaguely. What happened?"

"Remember the guy who disappeared that night? It was all over the news? They kept sending out search parties and he washed up along the river a few weeks later?"

"Oh my God, that's right. They said he was probably drunk and had wandered off, fell down a cliff, couldn't get up and was swept away. They weren't sure how he got there or where he got the booze. Was he at that party? With us?"

"I met him there that night. He was passing through town, heard about the party. He didn't know anyone. He was cute. I wanted him to feel welcome."

She snorted at the irony.

"You knew him? You never said anything?"

"I was with him when he died."

"You were . . . "

"We were so drunk. He was walking me home, along River Road. We were acting silly. He tripped and tumbled down this steep bank. I didn't know what was happening. I didn't know what to do. It was so dark."

I pulled my chair closer and took her in my arms; she had started whimpering like a child. "Oh, Car . . . "

"I did a terrible thing."

"It's not your fault."

"I was so drunk, and if they found out, I'd lose my scholarship. The church is so strict about things like that. I couldn't afford tuition. I would've had to drop out." She was trembling now, her face buried in my shoulder. I had no words to soothe.

Several minutes passed. "Addie, I left him to die alone. I never told anyone. He could have been saved."

"You don't know that."

"He kept calling my name; calling for help. I could hear him. I started running until I couldn't hear him any more."

"Oh my God. Is that what these letters are all about?"

"But I kept hearing him for weeks after that, even after they found his body. And then I didn't. But it's starting again. He's calling me in my dreams. I can't sleep."

"Who knows about this?"

"No one. That's what's so terrifying."

"Then who's writing these letters?"

"I don't know. Honest. I don't know."

"You never told anyone? Not Doyle? Your minister? A friend? A therapist? Your parents? Someone? Anyone? Are you sure?"

"Not one person. Not a soul. I swear to God."

We looked at each other. I saw the fear in her eyes. Or maybe she was reflecting my own fear back at me.

IT'S AMAZING HOW WE CAN STUFF tragedy into the deepest recesses of our minds and still live life as "normal" people. I guess it's called compartmentalization. You suffer abuse as a child and grow up to become a Mother Theresa. Or you abandon a boy to his death, and end up on TV, a beautiful, top-rated anchor bound for network glory.

Or you can listen as your friend tells you how she walked away from someone pleading for his life, and then spend the day with her, laughing and screaming your lungs out on a roller coaster.

That's exactly what happened after our conversation. We went to the Mall of America and forgot everything in the chaos of a Christmas-shopping crowd—by taking advantage of last-minute sales, eating lunch at the Rainforest Cafe, riding the scariest rides in the theme park, and pretending we were kids again.

We got back about five, time enough to shower and change before the guys came home—clomping through the door, one behind the other, cherry-cheeked and drippy-nosed, exuding good health and cold air. My eyes found Mark's and settled, and it seemed he was searching for me too. Anya, who took the night off to be with friends, had set out hot chocolate, egg nog and Christmas cookies, which we nibbled on and sipped until the pizza guy came.

By eight, four large pizzas, two six packs of beer, all of the egg nog and most of the cookies were history. We had moved into the den, around a Christmas tree that filled half the room and was loaded down with nineteenth century ornaments, as well as costume jewelry, fruits, and candy.

A robust fire crackled in the big stone fire place. We plopped down in chairs and opened our gifts. I gave Doyle and Caroline a view from my window, painted in oils. They gave me an art book on the Dutch Masters. Orin's gift was a bottle of vintage wine; Mark's, a cognac with a fancy French name I still can't pronounce. They each received a pair of Gordini ski gloves, which, they gushed, was exactly what they wanted.

Then we turned off the lights and sat in the glow of a raging fire that lulled us into silence. Caroline seemed drunk, which was unusual because she rarely drank; and, as far as I could tell, had been sipping cocoa most of the night. She and Doyle sat on the love seat, where he tried pulling her closer into a cuddle. But she shook him off, looking disgusted, continuing to sip from her marble-blue mug. Doyle looked defeated.

A-ha. Trouble in paradise

Something was wrong, but I didn't know what. I wondered if Anya and Doyle were having an affair; or if it was just a one-sided crush on Anya's part. I wondered if Caroline knew. I wondered if she was sneaking drugs or booze behind our backs.

I wondered about Orin, a guy who was dumped by his fiancée and betrayed by his best friend, yet laughs it off. Is that possible? I'd catch him glaring at Caroline one moment and trying to make her laugh the next.

I wondered about Mark, who wore no wedding ring, never mentioned a girlfriend, or children, or alimony payments and was beginning to look—after my third beer—like Michelangelo's *David*. I wondered when I'd last had sex, and when I couldn't come up with the answer, I felt even more deprived and abused.

I wondered if Caroline still kept a diary, which had been a sacred rite for her since she was a kid. She wrote in it everyday, detail after boring detail, every feeling, every person, every event, ad nauseum, late into the night. Maybe it had answers to some of my questions. Maybe not. I wondered what to do about those letters she received and whether it was a prank or a warning to be taken seriously.

Just then, a telephone rang several rooms away, causing Doyle to mumble, "Oh shit!" He set down his glass and struggled off the sofa, using Caroline's knee for balance—which irritated her.

He came back a few minutes later looking sheepish. "Boss's orders," he explained, and that he'd be back by morning. We urged him on his way, assuring him it was okay – he had a job to do.

I realized how sleepy I was. The booze, the fire, the warmth, the darkened room, the jet lag, the peace and the quiet—all coalesced to form one overwhelming sleeping pill. I could barely keep my eyes open. Mark and Orin looked just as tired.

But Doyle's departure brought Caroline back to life and she forced us, with slurring words and stumbling steps, to play *Pictionary*, which energized us for awhile. She and Orin made up one team; Mark and I another, which meant sitting close, touching, sharing . . . *possibilities*.

As an art major, I helped us take the lead. When I got the word *Iron*, however, I drew iron bars, a mine, a fist, the iron curtain—which no one could figure out. When they told me I could have drawn an "iron," I groaned. *Of course! So obvious!* I was more tired than I thought.

So I excused myself and headed for the stairs. Caroline came after me, a bit wobbly on her legs. She grabbed my hand and kept thanking me, her words garbled and slow. "You came. I'm so grateful. You are a good friend." She hugged me. Then she whispered, "I think I know what's going on. I know who sent those letters. Let's talk tomorrow."

I'd be leaving at noon to make a two-thirty flight, so we decided to meet in the dining room again between ten and ten-thirty.

Just then Mark and Orin emerged from the den. Mark saw me on the stairs, caught and held my eye, a question in there somewhere; but I was too tired to figure it out. *Hell! Our timing is so bad.* I turned to walk upstairs. The men headed for the kitchen.

When I reached the top, I looked back at Caroline who was watching them leave, her hand covering her mouth, figuring something out. Maybe she was confused. Or wondering what to do next. Or maybe she had reached some conclusion.

I'll never know.

* * *

I CALLED HANK WHEN I REACHED MY ROOM. It was after eleven there, but that was okay. When the rest of the world goes to sleep, he's waking up. Hank is my ex-husband and best friend. He plays saxophone for the *High Jinx*, a jazz band popular in pubs and clubs along Monterey's Cannery Row.

"Hey Babe."

"I thought you'd be playing tonight."

"Nah, it's Christmas Eve. Gotta take a night off once in awhile."

"How's Olivia?"

"She misses you. She whines every time I walk through the door, thinking it's you. A typical woman, never satisfied, good at laying on the guilt."

"I hear Roberta Flack in the background. Who is she tonight?"

"Bonnie, Betty, Beverly. I can't remember. She likes my sax."

"I *bet* she does."

And this is exactly why our marriage failed. Hank was adored by women who loved boyish-looking, soulful musicians. And he simply loved women who adored him—for whatever reason. After putting up with his philandering for a year, I filed for divorce. That's when we realized we were better off as friends. Without the tension of sex, we brought out the best in each other. Whatever happened, I knew Hank would have my back.

"You wouldn't believe how cold it is up here."

"It hit fifty-eight here. Sunshine all day long."

"Oh shut up!"

"How's it going?"

"This is a strange place.

"Yeah?"

I told him about the gingerbread house with a roof that looks like a witch's hat and a college friend who is beautiful and successful and seems to have a perfect life, but doesn't, really; who has few friends, and must share her home with a Nazi-maid hired by a husband who may or may not be faithful, who defends Russian mafia members and is still friends with a man she dumped.

"Is this making sense?"

"It sounds like the beginning of a bad novel I wouldn't finish—too ridiculous to be true."

"I swear to you, it's true. And besides, I'm not a writer. I'm a painter."

"No, I believe you. As they say, truth really is stranger than . . . ."

"Yeah, yeah . . . but here's the weirdest part."

Then I told him about the threatening letters Caroline had received and how no one knew what happened that Halloween night except the guy who fell down the cliff, and he was dead. And why she couldn't tell anyone back then and why it would ruin her reputation even now.

"She wants my help. I don't know what to tell her. What would you do, Hank?"

He took his time answering. "Listen. I can grab a red eye and be there in four hours. This isn't a safe place. Can you leave? Stay at a hotel?"

"See? This is why I always need a getaway car! You just never know when you have to get away!"

"Huh?"

"Never mind. I'm leaving tomorrow. I think it's safe until then. It's Caroline I worry about. She might have figured it out. That's what she said tonight, anyway. But she's not herself. She's had nothing to drink, but she seems bombed out of her head. Or maybe it's an act. Or she's really a druggie. I don't know. It's just weird. I'll be talking to her tomorrow morning before I leave. Maybe that'll explain everything. Maybe it's nothing at all . . . "

"I don't know, Babe."

"No, really. I feel better already—just talking to you."

"Yeah, that's my gift."

I chuckled. "You know what I mean!"

We confirmed when he'd be picking me up at the airport. He urged me again to leave and find a hotel. I assured him I'd be okay. But I was having a hard time staying awake and told him I had to go.

"Give Olivia a kiss for me."

"Slurp. Slurp."

"And give my best to Betty Boob. Or Beverly. Or . . .

" . . . 'Bye."

"You too."

"And Addie?"

"Yeah?"

"Lock your door."

So I did. Then I fell onto the bed belly first and was asleep in seconds. I sunk into some dark, velvety place where someone whimpered and was shushed and a car door slammed far away and witches' hats and headless men danced, smiling, all through a gingerbread house.

I woke up on Christmas day with a dry mouth, needles in my eyes, sand in my head, rocks in my stomach, and a vow never to drink again. It was the worst hangover I ever had. After showering and packing, I headed downstairs for coffee, aspirin, and a chance to talk with Caroline. On the way, I saw Doyle in the den, tearing pages from a book and tossing them into the fireplace. He was wearing last night's clothes, so I assumed he had just come from the office.

"'Mornin,'" he said when he saw me. "Just trying to keep this blaze going." Seeing my puzzlement, he added. "Oh! We try to conserve. Instead of throwing paper away, we use it for the fire."

I left him alone to save the planet and entered the dining room to find another huge breakfast waiting, but no Caroline. I drank a cup of coffee, then another, then a third and she still hadn't come down. I checked with Doyle, who said yesterday was tough on her, and she was probably sleeping late.

At eleven, I brought my suitcase out to the car, hoping to save time. And that's when I found her . . . .

The police arrived minutes later, swarming the house like black and white bees, herding everyone into the dining room and blocking off certain areas with yellow tape. When Doyle came back from rousing Mark and Orin, he carried the four letters sent to Caroline—which should have surprised me, but didn't. He kept insisting someone should read them, but was told to wait. "This is who did it," he'd said to anyone who'd listen. "This is the person you should be looking for."

Eventually a police woman took my statement, her expression bland, even when I told her what I knew. Then we sat and waited for the detectives. Doyle seemed bereft, covering his face and rubbing his eyes as if rousing himself from a bad dream, the envelopes laid out on the table, like a winning hand. Orin and Mark looked stunned, or hung over; I couldn't tell. Neither said anything. Mark avoided my eyes. Anya stood by the buffet, her arms crossed, her foot tapping, letting us know she had better things to do.

I was the first one called to the den.

Detective McBride was a heavy set, fifty-ish man with a hang-dog face and resigned expression, as if nothing could surprise him any more. He got angry when I showed him the tassel, said I could be arrested for interfering with a crime scene and obstructing justice, both felonies when murder was involved. But he calmed down when I told him the rest. At the end, I didn't know if he wanted to kill me or kiss me.

When Doyle and Anya were arrested that evening, I knew I'd done the right thing.

THE MURDER OF BEAUTIFUL CAROLINE Packard and the arrest of her attorney husband and his mistress made headlines for weeks—even reaching the San Francisco *Chronicle*.

After the autopsy, the guilty pleas, the sentencing, the dotting of the i's and crossing of the t's, Detective McBride called to tell me the full story.

He asked if I'd ever heard of Russian mystic Rasputin and said Anya had the same *voo-doo* power over Doyle.

"Anya wanted what Mrs. Packard had," McBride said. "She planned it; he did the grunt work. The dope! Lawyers are even dumber than I thought."

Not interested in his editorials, I brought him back to the news at hand. "So what happened?"

Apparently, Anya had spiked our cocoa to knock us out for the night. She knew Caroline, who didn't like liquor, would drink most of it, but—to make sure—coated her marble-blue mug with a chemical the police lab was still trying to identify.

"When her potions didn't work," McBride said, "she had Packard finish her off with a pillow."

"So Doyle didn't go to work after all?"

"Oh he went to work all right, but not to *work*."

Apparently, Doyle signed in at one-fifteen a.m., greeting Alex, the guard, and complaining about having to work on Christmas. Minutes later, however, Doyle snuck down the back stairs and exited through a door few people knew about. He walked to the end of the block, where Anya picked him up and drove him back home to do the deed.

"But why did they put her body in my car? Why me?"

"Anya didn't like you, pure and simple. She thought this would set you up as the prime suspect and make your life miserable for awhile."

"But wouldn't they know that doesn't make sense? I couldn't carry her myself, and the autopsy would reveal . . . "

"Yeah, well, she's a nut job. And he's a defense lawyer. We know what idiots they . . . "

"So after killing Caroline, they drove back to his office and . . . "

"Good old Alex said he saw him sign out about six in the morning. He wished Packard a merry Christmas and claimed the poor guy 'looked whipped'. My ass! The poor jerk was being set up as Packard's alibi."

Then McBride begrudgingly acknowledged my help in his investigation.

After I saw Doyle in the den tearing out those pages, I soon realized he'd sent the letters. That *ledger* was Caroline's diary. She never told anyone about her secret, but I'm sure she wrote about it in her diaries. Apparently, Anya found them in a safe box hidden in the back of her closet.

And that meant the person (or persons) who read those diaries had to be responsible for the threatening letters. It was a form of misdirection that Doyle hoped would take the spotlight off *the husband,* and focus it elsewhere—for a long time to come.

And when I'd seen Doyle in the den, I realized something was out-of-kilter—which is hard to explain, because you have to be an artist to understand. We see the world differently. For us, it's all about shapes, colors, composition, balance, lights, shadows, empty space. So when I saw Doyle, the picture was *off* somehow. I figured out why, but didn't know its importance until later: a tassel was missing on his left loafer.

The police salvaged bits and pieces of the diary from the fireplace and showed them to Doyle, along with his missing tassel. It ultimately "did him in," McBride said. But not right away. Since I took the tassel from the murder scene, they couldn't use it as evidence. But Doyle didn't know that. When they told him it was laying next to Caroline's body, he clammed up and asked for his lawyer.

When they showed it to Anya, however, and told her Doyle had confessed, she said, "Is too bad. You gonna need more for to arrest *me*." So they gave her two choices: tell the truth, or be sent back to Russia. Turns out, she'd rather spend her life in an American jail than return to her homeland. Anya folded like a cheap lawn chair and brought Doyle down with her.

"You did good," McBride said. "Didn't think so at the time, but you did."

After more small talk and some awkward silences, we ended the call.

I hung up, hugged my dog and breathed in the smell of fresh bread from the bakery below.

"She didn't like me?"

* * *

I'M NOT LUCKY IN LOVE EITHER, EVEN WHEN I think it's falling into my lap. For example, I thought Mark and I had made a connection, so I called him after the first of the year. We shared memories of sweet Caroline, then talked about our strange Christmas in Minnesota, the indignities of air travel, the weather.

"I'd like to see you again," I finally said. "What do you think?"

I waited for a response, but didn't get one. My stomach slid up into my throat.

"Boulder isn't that far. I hear it's beautiful. I'd love to see it one of these weekends. Or maybe you could come here. Carmel is gorgeous—by the sea?"

"Addison."

"Call me Addie."

"Addie, I have to tell you . . . I'm involved right now, *very* involved."

"Oh, I didn't know. I'm sorry. I tend to leap before I look. Sorry. She's a lucky lady, whoever she is. What's her name?"

"It's not a her. It's a he. He's a he. Joshua."

"Oh. Omi . . . Well, good for you. I *really* didn't know. That's great! Some of my best friends . . . ."

Fortunately, thank God, we both started laughing.

We chit-chatted some more, solved the world's problems and hung up—him with an invitation to bring Joshua down here for a visit, me with an invitation to bring whomever up to Boulder.

I slumped down in the couch, where Olivia – all fifty-two pounds of her – jumped up to claim her place in my lap. She gave me that big button-eyed look she knows I can't resist. I grabbed her furry face, kissed the top of her head and told her, "Okay. So I'm good at landscapes. Men not so much."

She schlurped my face and waggled her tail in agreement.

This would have to do. For now.

Kathleen Lindstrom sold her soul for 25 years to corporate America as a writer in communications, marketing, & public relations. Six years ago, however, she finally delved into the world of creative fiction. Since then she has won the Arthur Edelstein Prize for Short Fiction and three honorable mentions in other competitions. Her short stories have appeared in seventeen magazines, literary anthologies, and e-zines. Her poem "Shrapnel" won first place in the 2007 *Talking Stick* competition. Kathleen recently completed her first novel, *The Light Gets In,* and is seeking a publisher.

Check-Out at Ten

J. Henry

A PAIR OF HEADLIGHTS CHASED the two-lane ribbon of snow through powdered conifers and naked birch. Without signaling, the boatish sedan turned into the isolated parking lot at the Whispering Winds Motel. It slid to a halt against a freshly shoveled mound of white fluff. Dwarfed by a stand of seventy-year white pines, two figures emerged from the '88 Cadillac.

Inside, Sharla sat behind the age-honeyed, knotty pine desk, head back, eyes closed, oblivious to the movements outside. Not a feature twitched when the screen door smacked against the flaking doorjamb. Nor did she stir when Miss Evelyn shuffled loudly toward the desk, her white-haired paramour in tow.

"I need a room. King-size with hot tub, away from the ice machine, view of the lake, and smoking."

Sharla tilted forward like a ragdoll. Her parted black bangs closed like curtains across her forehead. One aquamarine eye opened to gauge this intrusion barking orders as if they'd entered the Waldorf-Astoria rather than a rodent-ridden dive in Nordkapp, Minnesota, three miles shy of Ontario. She judged the lopsided couple to be a step ahead of the Reaper as they oscillated in and out of focus.

The squat woman with a silvery gray bun, generous figure, and dressed in a frightful print, stared while her taller fellow, clad in a moth-frayed remnant of a natty smoking jacket, bobbed in her wake, whistling an aimless tune. Sharla's slouch intact, she responded. "Got one double with shower, ice is broke, can't see the lake for the drifts, and no smoking. Take it or pack it."

A loud thud jerked Sharla upright in her chair. A suitcase of a purse dominated her field of vision.

"How much?" Miss Evelyn asked as she rooted for her wallet.

Like cracks chasing weakened ice across the lake, a frown messed with Sharla's barely twenty-year old features.

"There a problem?" the elder enquired.

"No, no, everything's ...," Sharla plucked a form from a stack at her side while her eyes drifted like a Sunday afternoon, "... wonderful."

Drugs, concluded Miss Evelyn. How sad. Shakily, she filled in her essentials on the form. Her gaze dropped to the dress she had crafted from old drapes, a Christmas present to herself. Festooned with bright palms and knotted green vines on a red background, the holiday colors cheered her while the theme made her feel sultry and carnivorous, a pent up beast in a lush jungle.

Miss Evelyn's glance ventured sidelong at her other Christmas present. What was his name again? Oh, the things that slipped through her head these days. Robert? Roland? Roquefort? Goodness no, she thought. That's a cheese. Stilton! There it was. Robert Stilton. She noticed then the robust Viagra-tent accessorizing Robert's tired jacket and noisy holiday tie. Good Lord, only four hours left!

Miss Evelyn hurriedly handed over her completed form, silently praising Bob Dole for proselytizing God's gift to women. "Key please," she said. "I'm in a rush."

"Holy Moses!" Sharla shrieked.

Miss Evelyn stumbled back, startled, and nearly toppled Mr. Stilton. "Good gracious, dear, what on earth is the matter?"

Sharla looked up innocently and shrugged. She exhaled loudly and said as she checked off boxes on the form, "Yeah, right there, and there." She let loose a deep sigh. "He with you?"

"He is." Miss Evelyn leaned in conspiratorially and winked. "But just for tonight."

"Mmmm, that's yummy." Sharla spun the form to Miss Evelyn. "He's another twelve bucks. Check out at ten. Sign here."

"You sure you're all right?" Miss Evelyn asked.

"Oh, yeah ..." Sharla lifted a key from a rack of hooks but stalled mid-air, her eyes focused somewhere distant. Miss Evelyn reached for the dangling key but Sharla kept jerking her hand as her guest grabbed for the prize like a trout trailing a shiny spinner. Suddenly, Sharla slammed the key on the counter. As another load groan escaped, the door behind her flew open with a deafening report.

Miss Evelyn screamed.

A loud thump sounded under the desk and Sharla fell off her chair to the floor. A round young man with a knit cap and dressed like a lumberjack burst through the open door, a light bulb cradled in one hand. "Sharla!"

From under the desk, another young man crawled out, this one dressed in a red waffle shirt, torn jeans, and thick socks. "Jesus Christ, Oscar. You scared the crap out of me." He swiped his wrist across his soul patch then rubbed his shaggy blond head. "Dang, I hit my head."

Miss Evelyn, working her jaw but unable to muster sound, snatched the key, then her date, and fled.

Oscar watched Billy tuck in his shirt and Sharla right herself. He fingered a pocketful of coins as she straightened her skirt.

"What?" Sharla snapped.

"Someone died," Oscar said.

"Oh, my God, Oscar. Who?"

"I don't know. There's a funny smell in room ten. I went in to change the bulb in the desk lamp. Smells like when Uncle Zig died."

Billy harrumphed and grabbed a candy bar from the shelf of sundries on the back wall. "Aw, probably some alkie blew cookies." He laughed. "From both ends."

Sharla smacked his arm. "Billy, this is serious." She looked over the guest register. "Now that I think of it, the guy should have checked out this morning. Maybe he's hurt."

"You know what?" Billy said. "I bet those yahoos in room eight are cooking something on that frickin' Coleman again. I bet that's what he smelled." Billy leaned in to Sharla's ear. "Besides, Oscar's a retard. What does he know from smells?"

She smacked him again. "Don't use the 'R' word."

"Should we call the cops?" Oscar asked. "I like the cops."

"At least someone's thinking." Sharla grabbed the phone as she pushed Billy away. "Good idea."

Billy paced behind the counter watching Sharla get sucked away from their little situation into a more crowded one. He slammed the desk with his hand. "Damn it! Why don't these people ever go to the Holiday Inn?"

Sharla held up the receiver. "Phone's dead."

"Oh, yeah." Oscar said. "They're fixing the broken poles from the ice storm."

"Great." Sharla plopped into her chair. After a thoughtful minute, she swiveled. "Billy?" She rubbed his leg with her fuzzy-socked foot.

He moved closer. "Yeah?"

"Sexy Billy ... do me a big, huge favor?"

"With Oscar here?"

Her foot inched up his thigh. "No, no. Not that. Go with Oscar and see what's up in ten. Then we can finish 'that' ... later."

"Go with...?" His shoulders sagged from love's burden. "But we were busy." He brushed her cheek and tried his puppy-eyes. "I was just getting started."

Sharla fanned her face with Miss Evelyn's registration form. "I know, Baby. Believe me, I know. But I can't leave the desk. Daddy'll kill me." She took Billy's hand and kissed it. "Please?" Her lashes fluttered above a smile shaped to motivate. Her lips circled Billy's fingertip and pulled back with a wet pop. "I'll make it worth your while."

Billy's eyes widened, a lot. He slipped his feet into unlaced snowmobile boots, dashed around the counter, and pushed Oscar out the door. "Time's a-wasting, my friend. Let's check out this skanky stink."

THE DUO WALKED BRISKLY PAST WEATHER-PATINATED doors strung along the covered walk. Snow crunched with every footfall. Party sounds overflowed from room two. In five, a T.V. bellowed a used-car commercial while rhythmic grunts in room six broadcast untamed urgency.

Oscar stopped. "Billy? What were you doing under the desk?"

Billy kept moving. "Talking."

"You guys sure talk a lot."

Billy copped a quick look back at the office. "Not nearly enough, you ask me."

A hint of the next round of weather whispered from the northwest and rattled the unlatched screen door to room ten. "Hold your nose," Oscar said.

Billy slid a wrinkled pack of smokes from his chest pocket and scratched a match to a cigarette. "I saw this on TV once. Covers the smell." He pulled the screen door and pounded on the heavy green door. Nothing.

Oscar stepped up and unlocked the door, then stepped back. "You first."

With a cautious twist of his wrist, Billy pushed the door open. A piquant odor tickled his nose. "Man, who died in here?" Billy said.

Oscar peeked in. "I don't see any dead people."

"It's a joke, Einstein. There's definitely something funky, but I don't think anyone died." Billy stepped into the room. "Did you set a mousetrap or something?"

"All the rooms have mousetraps."

"Well, there you go. Where is it?"

Oscar pointed. "Under the bed."

As he passed it, Billy studied the open suitcase displaying crisply folded dress shirts in business blue and ecru. A well-worn leather briefcase sat squarely on the nearby desk, manila folders stacked precisely on top.

"Sure is neat," Oscar noted.

Billy tapped his forehead. "Depressive-impulsive. A neat-freak." He got on his knees and lifted the overhanging bedspread. "Whoa," he said as he slid out a well-decayed white rat, its front legs and snout clamped in the small wire trap. "I smell a rat."

Oscar gasped. "Oh, my goodness!"

"I know, it's a big honker, isn't it? Hey, remember that couple from the Cities who lost their pet rat a few weeks ago? This must be Ralph!" Billy held out his cigarette and laughed. "Hello, Ralph. Wanna smoke?"

"Oh, my goodness," Oscar said again, this time choked with anxiety.

"Relax, man. He's dead. I'll get rid of him." Billy stood with the tail-end of the dangling rodent pinched in his outstretched fingers. "There's a big hole in the wall under the—"

"Billy!"

Billy turned. "What, Oscar, what?"

Oscar pointed into the bathroom. His face had drained of color.

More curious than concerned, Billy walked to the bathroom. Oscar tended to be squeamish about the littlest things. Oscar leaned over Billy's shoulder as he peered in. "Oh, Jesus," Billy bellowed. "Back up, back up. Jesus Christ."

As at any roadside mattress-stop, the bathroom was a closet. The toilet faced the sink and the tub stretched alongside both. Bisecting this grouping, a hairy male body laid ass-up over the tub side, tangled in the shower curtain, his legs slung to the floor. His pants and underwear collected around black Florsheims. A crimson stripe streaked over the mallards flying across the curtain. A swirl of scarlet seeped lazily from his head in a foot of water.

"This is not good, Oscar," Billy said. "Not good at all."

Oscar crossed himself. "He's dead."

"Gee, ya think? Man, look at all that blood." His eyebrows lifted as a thought took wing. "Hey, you think he offed himself? Maybe a bullet to the head or something?"

Oscar, suddenly itchy, moved his cap around. "I don't see a gun."

Billy looked behind the toilet, under the sink, and in the tub. "You're right. No gun." When he stood, he noticed Oscar pushing his pinky into a small hole next to the door. "What'd you find?" He squeezed Oscar out of the way and kneeled. "Dude! A bullet hole." He traced his finger around the quarter-inch circle, cut cleanly through the cold ceramic. Billy looked back at the tub. "Whoa." He stretched his arms in a straight line from hole to body. "He was shot from next door."

"How do you know that?" Oscar asked.

"Good old-fashioned police work," Billy said as he tossed his spent cigarette into the toilet. "See the trajectory? Nowhere else it could come from." He thought a moment. "Had to have been an accident, though. Imagine, you're sittin' on the shitter minding your own business, then 'BAM!' Lights out in London. Wouldn't that just suck?"

Billy suddenly jumped to his feet and walked out of the room.

"Where you going?" Oscar followed and found Billy pacing around the bed, pointing wildly at the door.

"We have to go next door," Billy said. "I bet there's a matching hole in that bathroom."

"What if he's in there? The bad guy, I mean."

Billy stopped, his hand on the doorknob. "Hmmm, good point. He may not be a bad guy though. Maybe he's just an idiot. No offense."

Oscar looked at the bathroom. "I don't think he can hear you from the other room."

"No, no, I meant ..." Billy stopped, rolled his eyes. "Listen, let's ask Sharla if he's in."

He exploded from the room and nearly decked Sharla coming down the walkway cloaked in an open fleece-lined coat. "Hey," he said as he helped Sharla regain balance. "Who's in room twelve?"

She straightened her sleeve. "Why? What did you find?"

"Oscar was right. There's a stiff in the tub."

"And he's dead," Oscar said.

Sharla paled. "Seriously? Oh my God. That salesman?"

"And there's a rat," Oscar added.

"What? Who?"

"Ralph."

"Who's Ralph?"

"Remember?" Billy said. "Missing rat? Couple weeks ago? We found him too. Must have been crawling through the walls then chewed his way out, right into a trap. Anyway, who's next door?"

Sharla thought a moment. "Let's see, room twelve ... oh, yeah, some schmuck-husband sampling a side dish. Why?"

"Is he in?" Billy asked.

"I think he left a while ago, but I'm not sure." She smiled. "I was a little distracted, you know."

He pulled her close. "Oh yeah..."

"But what's he got to do with the dead guy?" Sharla asked.

Billy let go of her and looked blankly at the sky. "Not sure yet, but I have a theory."

"Oh, no you don't, Billy Boyd. No more theories. Remember? Listen, I borrowed a cell phone from one of the guests. She actually has coverage here. Anyway, I came to tell you I called the cops."

Billy stopped and faced her. "Well hell, that's great. Meanwhile, it'll only take them all day to get here. As long as the room's empty we should check for evidence..." Billy looked around and said softly, "... of foul play."

"Oh, brother."

"Come on, Shar. Just a quick peek? The killer might get away."

"Now there's a killer?" She folded her arms. "Absolutely not. You promised you wouldn't act on any more wild notions."

"This is different. It's serious, like you said."

"Different?" Sharla said. "Different like when you thought my mom was having an affair?"

Billy looked away from her. "How was I supposed to know your uncle was visiting?"

"Different like those newlyweds you thought tried to burn down the motel?"

Billy quickly dropped a freshly-lit cigarette and ground it out with his foot. "Yeah, I know. It was my ash in the garbage. Still, it wasn't me who threw the paper in the—"

"Different like when you thought Oscar was dying of cancer when he shaved his head?"

Billy laughed, "Okay, I admit. That was dumb." He patted Oscar's head. "But I sure raised a ton of money, didn't I, Oscar?"

"Sharla's right," Oscar said. "Wait for the cops."

Billy threw his hands in the air. "Come on you guys. The killer's going to get away."

"Let the police handle it," Sharla said. "I've got work to do. So do you." She started off, but the door at room six creaked open.

"Young lady?"

They all turned and saw Miss Evelyn's head and torso leaning out. Her black bustier looked about to burst. "I need help with a knot."

"Aw, man." Billy rolled his eyes. "What next?"

Sharla elbowed him hard. "Take a pill, would ya?" She headed toward Miss Evelyn, but stopped. She glared at Billy. "Don't do anything stupid."

"Yeah, yeah." Billy leaned against the wall. He tapped the back of his head against the cold wall. "No one gets me." His heels bounced nervously, left then right, tap, tap, tap. Then he stopped. "Hey, did she just call me stupid?"

Suddenly Sharla stepped out and called to Billy. He jumped a foot in the air. "What? I didn't do anything."

"F.Y.I., I'm untying a necktie."

"A necktie. Wahoo. We have a murderer on the loose and she's helping an old guy get naked. Why can't I have a necktie so I can find a nice old tree and hang myself?" He lit another cigarette and threw the match. "I can't stand this. Let's go."

"Where are we going?" Oscar asked.

Billy started walking. "Plan B."

"You have a Plan B?" Oscar shook his head as he stomped on Billy's flaming match. "Uh oh."

BEHIND THE MOTEL, BILLY AND OSCAR high-stepped through dense clumps of dried grasses sprouting through twinkling white drifts under the moonlight. Billy counted down the row of high windows. Two deer bolted into the forest when they passed The Mound. A pile of rusted mattress frames, car tires, lumber, and other detritus.

"Here we are," Billy said, pointing at a rotting sash. "Room twelve. Look, the bathroom window's open a crack." He jumped up several times to look in but the sill was too high. "Give me a boost, would ya?"

Oscar saluted and made a hand-step.

Billy stepped and pulled up. "Damn, the windows fogged up. I can't see the hole. Hang on." He quietly raised the window as high as he could and without warning heaved himself through.

"Hey," Oscar yelled, "what are you doing?"

Billy poked his head out. "Shhh. Just a quick look-see. I'll be out in a--"

A veil of dread cloaked his face. He slowly retreated from the window and it slammed shut. Oscar stared in disbelief. When the window didn't open again, he leapt like a fawn through the pristine wonderland, screaming for Sharla.

BILLY LOOKED TO HIS SIDE AND DOWN. A beefy man in a Santa suit knelt at his feet. His sausage fingers firmly grasped a semi-automatic pistol aimed at Billy's crotch.

"Evening, dickhead," Santa offered by way of introduction. "So much as breathe and I blow your balls out your ass."

A warbling giggle floated from the other room. Billy shifted his gaze enough to see a thirtyish, red-haired woman lounging sidesaddle on the bed. An amber drink rested on her thigh, steadied by her red and green-nailed fingers. He tried without success to not stare at her streetwalker-elf outfit. His eyes locked on her black stiletto heels then followed her fishnet legs up to her short green silk skirt with white fur trim. A matching green top with all the trimmings, low-buttoned and taut, and a down-turned pointy hat with a dangling white fur-ball made the costume at once comely and distressing to Billy's addled mind. She winked at Billy and laughed again, spilling her drink on the bed sheet.

"Oh, foo," she said and slid away from the stain. Her gut-laugh ricocheted through the rooms. "Look, Honey. This time I made the wet spot."

"Hey, that's cute Wanda." Santa chuckled. "Now shut up."

His ice-blue eyes drilled Billy. "Okay, kid, show's over." He stood and backed away, revealing a sizable paunch straining his wide black belt. Santa motioned toward the bedroom with his gun. "Move."

"Who? Me?"

"No, the dumbshit behind you."

Billy turned to look.

"Jesus." Santa shook his head and pushed Billy toward the bed. Under the guidance of the pointed pistol, Billy sat on the mattress edge, anxious about Wanda lurking behind him.

Santa grabbed a wooden desk chair from the middle of the room and sat to face his captive. "So ... what?" he smirked. "My wife hire you to check on my extracurricular activities?"

Billy straightened. "You shot the guy next door."

Santa's eyebrows leapt. "Hey, now that's funny. Isn't that funny Wanda?" He leveled the gun at Billy. "Okay, cut the crap. What's going on?"

"Through the wall," Billy insisted. "You shot him through the bathroom wall."

"I never shot nobody. But--," he twirled his gun Old West-style, pointed it at Billy's head, and jerked his arm back from the imaginary re-coil, "--always a first time."

Billy felt a warm, wet trickle under his arm. It worsened when Wanda crawled around and touched his cheek. When he noticed that only her silky thin top separated his arm and her soft breast, a swarm of butterflies lofted in his belly.

"You've been a naughty elf," she cooed and stroked Billy's face with her fingers. He turned away, but catlike, Wanda slinked around and grabbed his face. She kissed him, sloppy, on the mouth. She kneeled on the bed next to him.

"I've been naughty, too," she said and crawled over his lap. She arched her bottom over his thighs and teased up her skirt. "But Santa's only going to spank me. He's going to fuck you up but good."

Santa guffawed and slapped her scantily laced behind so it jiggled. His expression clouded again. "Alright, Kid. I don't have all day. Tell me what the--"

The front door suddenly burst open and a police officer lunged in, following his drawn pistol.

"Freeze!"

Billy jumped up, hands high, rolling Wanda off his lap. She thudded to the floor with a curse. Santa calmly raised both hands, gun dangling loosely from his finger.

A towering khaki figure, the local Sheriff, stepped in after the officer. He quickly sized up the room. Noting the adrenaline-crazed eyes of his front-man, he reached over and lowered his subordinate's revolver. "Easy there, Olsen. Nothing going on here. It's just Billy."

Sheriff Carson walked over to Santa and retrieved the gun from his hooked finger. "I'll just hang on to this for a bit." He turned to Billy. A vein threatened to fracture Carson's closely shorn umber skull. "Billy," his voice boomed. "What part of freeze didn't you get? We God-damn near perforated your sorry ass."

Half an hour later, Sheriff Carson held up the wall outside room ten as Billy capped his rendition of the night's events. The Sheriff listened with amusement and nodded politely as he jotted notes in his dog-eared notepad.

"So I went next door to see who shot the guy in the tub. When I found that wing-nut in the Santa-suit flashing his hardware, I put two-and-two together." Billy pulled a cigarette from his pack with his lips, speaking as he lit up. "The poor slob in ten was probably getting ready for a nice warm bath when his neighbor started flashing his piece for his bimbo. Next thing you know, BAM! The bullet blasts through the wall. Dude's wasted. Case closed." Billy exhaled an opaque cloud, trying to conceal his smile. Clearly, brilliant detective work.

A patrolman came up behind Carson and tapped his shoulder. The officer whispered a stream of breath-fog in his ear. The Sheriff stifled a snicker when he finally broke free.

"What's so funny?" Billy asked.

Sheriff Carson rubbed his temples. "You know, this morning I stopped by the diner and talked to your mother. She asked me if I had something to keep you out of trouble this winter after the holidays. By the way, how is your Dad doing? He up and walking yet?"

Billy shook his head and exhaled a grey plume. "Nah. Another couple weeks, doctor says."

"Terrible thing. Terrible. Damn snowmobiles." The Sheriff looked at the sky, lost in thought. A laden sigh escaped. "Anyway, I thought, sure, I have a couple cases that could use a little help in the legwork department. They'd be perfect for you--no thinking, nothing dangerous, just errands. But Jesus, Billy, now I don't know. This is easily the most goofy-assed of all the goofy-assed states of affairs you've ever masterminded."

"But I solved the—"

"Whoa, hotshot, you didn't solve anything. You only pissed off a union boss from Thunder Bay who's a pinch and a poke away from a broken marriage, but that's none of our business." He shook his head. "So, here's how it's stacking up, and based on preliminary evidence, we're about ninety-nine percent square on what happened here. Follow me, please."

A variety of uniforms occupied room ten. Sheriff Carson paged through his pad as he entered. He pointed his pen at the bathroom. "Our expired guest, Mr. James Francis Havilland, a siding peddler, was getting ready last night, as you correctly deduced, for a quiet soak after a grueling day on the road."

He lifted a Bible lying on top of an open phone book.

"Looks like he was going to order pizza, do his nightly devotions, then hit the sheets."

Billy followed into the bathroom and bumped into the Sherriff when he stopped.

"Easy, boy, you're squashing me."

Billy let the Sheriff fill the room with his gestures.

"So James is in the potty unpacking his toiletries and checks the water in the tub. Too hot. Okey doke, change in plans." The Sheriff looked in the toilet, grimaced, shut the lid, and sat. "So he takes a dump instead while the water cools. With business concluded, he stands up." Carson rose. "Bends over to hoist his trousers and SMACK!" He slapped the sink with his pad, "whacks his forehead on the sink. It is kind of cozy in here."

Billy nodded, trying to keep up. He pulled out his cigarette pack.

"By the way," Carson said. "I can't seem to figure out why a cigarette would be in the toilet. Any thoughts?"

Billy looked at the pack in his hand and quickly returned it to his shirt pocket. "Nope," he said.

"So he's knocked senseless, teeters, and falls against the shower curtain into the tub. Summation: he drowned. Any way you slice it, Billy, it's a crappy way to go, no pun intended, but it wasn't murder."

Billy looked around the room in disbelief. How could he have missed all those details? Suddenly he didn't feel so good.

"One thing I can't figure out," the Sheriff continued. "You said that dead rat's smell is what got Oscar's attention. How could the deceased not notice that?"

Billy thought about that. Then he remembered. "A cold! He had a cold. There was nose spray in his suitcase."

"A stuffy nose. Yeah, Billy. That's good. He couldn't smell anything. nice work."

Billy puffed up and remembered something else. "Hey, what about the bullet hole? There, by the door."

"Ah, yes. The bullet hole. Now that's another ponderable isn't it?" Sheriff Carson scratched his chin. "Let's look behind the door." He swung the bathroom door closed. "Here we find an identical hole about two feet away. About the length of a towel bar by my guess."

Billy thumped his forehead. "Oh, man. I took that out last spring. Duh."

Sheriff Carson scrutinized Billy a long minute. The ghost of himself thirty years back was hard to ignore; jazzed up, foolish, trying to escape the walls of adulthood pressing in. Lots of energy and ideas, but no place to put them. He had only needed a nudge to channel his energy toward something meaningful. Billy's grandfather, a Border Patrol officer, who lived across the street until he died a decade ago, had given the Sheriff more chances than he deserved to get his shit together.

Sheriff Carson was sure if he kept pushing Billy along, the young man would find a calling, just like he had. He owed the old man that much. With a sharp slap, he shut his pad and stuffed it into his jacket pocket. He put his arm around Billy's shoulder and they went outside to breathe in the crisp dawn.

"Duh indeed, Billy. Duh indeed."

J. Henry lives with his menagerie of family and pets in Minneapolis. "Don't quit your day job," as they say in the biz, so his alter ego works as an architect. Publications include short stories in *Metal Scratches* and a number of web-based short story collections. He has also received an Honorable Mention in the *Writer's Digest* Annual Short Fiction Contest. A memoir and novel are in the works.

As The Year Dies

T. J. Roth

KAINDA! WANT ME TO CALL the moving van for your stuff, or what?

I took one last look in the bathroom mirror at the mess of dark curls I'd been trying to tame. Giving up, I pulled the whole mess into a ponytail of sorts. "Very Jennifer-Beals-works-out," I told my mirror image. Although Flashdance was already eight years in the past, Ms. Beals had been a hero of my then-sixteen-year-old self.

Heavy snow had not only wreaked havoc with my hair, it'd also caused mascara stains. Not for the first time, I questioned my wisdom at using make-up given my job. Moving closer to the mirror, I swiped under each eye with a square of tissue, examining the hazel staring back at me.

"Yo! Kainda! You dead in there?" The voice belonged to my one-time FTO—field training officer—in the Minneapolis Police Department.

"Hang on, Sarge!"

I stood under the hand dryer for a few seconds, then grabbed my things and emerged from the Ladies somewhat more put together than I'd entered. Nonetheless when he saw me, Sergeant Vic Schulski smirked.

"What? You take a shower in your uniform in there?"

"Wise ass. You may not have noticed, but it's snowing gigantic globs. Chris and I were standing in it for hours busting Locos. Anyways, if I'da known you were out here waiting to pick me up, I woulda worn my ball gown."

He made a noise somewhere between a grunt and a gaffaw, and started walking down the hall. I trotted to catch up and then walked at his side. He continued, "Asked around about you, someone said you went in there. Like, ten minutes ago."

Vic was rock-armed and thick-chested. Other notable features included a blonde crew cut and blue eyes the exact color of our summer uniform shirts, with the beginnings of crinkles around them.

I said, "Never question a woman's time in the can, Sarge. It's how we stay so be-ay-oot-iful."

The crinkles deepened. Always fighting his taste for greasy foods, at six-one Vic probably fluctuated between 220 when all muscle, 235 when not. I poked him playfully in the abdomen. "Looks like someone forgot about the gym last week. Or is that all the Christmas cookies you've been scarfing?"

"I might be up an ounce or two since we last worked together. Speaking of which, got a potential opportunity for you. Interested?"

I stopped walking as we approached the door to the squad room and said, "Yeah, of course."

"Great. Head up in thirty."

"What? To the batcave?" I asked, organizing a mock look of shock on my face. "Gasp. A mere mortal like me? In the inner sanctum sanctorum?"

This earned a dramatic hands-on-hips, exasperated-school-principal pose.

Vic commanded the Street Crime unit. They worked plainclothes and street hours, and had their own squad room that no one else could enter. They worked mostly drugs and prostitution. Sometimes guns if citizens complained about that. Other times, the state investigation agency or Organized Crime unit asked them to work special projects. Sounded good to me.

I sing-songed, "Whatcha gonna do? Give me detention?"

He tried to keep the hard-ass look on his face, but his mouth twitched up on one side. Referring to my partner, he said, "Bring Hausen. And tell him to shape you up first."

I headed into the general squad room. "Fat chance, boss," I called. I didn't see, but knew he was shaking his head and watching my ass as I walked away.

I FOUND CHRIS HAUSEN IN THE SQUAD break-room with some guys who were laughing about our Christmas tree. Chris tended to not laugh or smile at work, but I knew him well and could see the amusement in his dark eyes.

The tree had been completely denigrated. Put up early in December by precinct secretaries—we still had them in the early nineties, none of us ever having heard of an "administrative assistant"—it had started out a white-lighted, silver-tinseled, candy-cane-bedecked thing of beauty in comparison to the general pig-sty decor.

About mid-month, someone had put fishing line through the handle of Officer Tony DeGroot's tit-shaped cup and hung it next to one of the candy canes with an inscription reading, "What Tony sucks on while he thinks of J & K." After that, Jill, the brand new rookie and only other woman uniform in our precinct, and I had stopped by Sex World and bought the tiniest, cheapest, realistic-style dildo we could find. We looped it by the balls with green ribbon, and hot-glued a long tag that read "Tony DeGroot's dick. Shown actual size. He has a better chance of the boys in 4th sucking it."

A naked Barbie who'd obviously been soaked in coffee or tea to make her appear just this side of ethnic, hence representing me, appeared the next day hot-glued from behind to a lily white Ken with his smile artificially widened and piece of toothpick creating the thumb for his "thumbs up" sign. Sick bastards, using their daughters' dolls and their wives' craft-room supplies that way. Anyway, after that things really got twisted.

Back then, any women on the MPD weren't in "Fours," what we called the Fourth Precinct for short. The north side. The bad side. The side yuppies from Kansas City, Omaha, and Sioux Falls didn't move to when they took their hot shit jobs downtown at American Express Financial Advisors or Dayton's Corporate or out in the suburbs at 3M or Pillsbury. It was a point of pride with me, and another rebellion against my parents, that I also lived in this precinct.

There were a few men who treated us with respect from day one, without making a big show of it. Jill and I called them "Fuckin' Good Guys," FuGGs for short. Vic was a fugg. Chris, the partner I got after Vic figured I was trained enough, was also a fugg. I suppose they gave us to the fuggs in order to avoid "issues."

After getting Chris away from the guys around the tree, I filled him in on our invite upstairs. With shaved bald head, red-brown goatee, and tending to smile only when he wasn't at work, Chris looked mean. The look worked for him, but I knew underneath he was a teddy bear. Anyone who saw him with three-year-old Chris Junior—C.J., or his wife Mandy knew that. He pushed six feet and was scary strong. At work he usually wore a cap, mostly backwards, often with his glasses planted above the brim. In winter, these hats only changed thickness. Another signature item was his broad gold wedding band. Very conspicuous. Very married, in addition to being a fugg—probably both good reasons to partner him with me.

He'd started with Raim, my sort-of-fiancée, at the MPD four years before I'd joined the force. He and his wife, Mandy-the-masters-student, and Raim and I had become great couple-pals since the brass partnered me with Chris. Mandy put up with a lot of our crap, and occasionally got us back by going on and on about details of her master's thesis, which had something to do with blending psychology and literature. She liked to talk about how aspects of our job were reflected in Shakespeare's tragedy plays. Actually, I had to admit that some of her arguments started to interest me in Shakespeare.

Great partner, hot almost-fiancée, and a job I loved. Life was good. I figured I was in for a job most women cops shrink from—dressing like a whore and walking Broadway on jump-outs, but I craved any experience. That is, that's what I figured until the minute Chris and I walked into the Street Crime batcave.

· ·

CAN YOU FUCKING BELIEVE THAT SHIT? They fucking put out a fucking manger scene in the fucking front yard!? With fucking Christmas lights around it? Fuck."

At his last curse, Officer Joey Toscano stood and started pacing. Toscano didn't take matters of faith lightly. Mid-height and solid, he was handsome with curly dark hair and dark eyes. Italian. Very Italian. Very Italian Catholic. The hard-swearing and hard-drinking kind.

Chris and I exchanged glances.

"That's sacrilegious," Matt "Itchy" Johnson murmured as Vic waved us in to join them. Itchy was hard to pin down. About five-seven, dark hair, thirty-five years old, so eleven years older than me and about Vic's age. He was wearing a plain long-sleeved grey T-shirt with a black stocking cap and jeans. The cap had a Harley logo on it. He looked like a hard-ass redneck thug in some ways, but on the other hand he could look clean cut. His intense face was almost handsome. Dark brows were dominant, giving him an aggressive look.

The first time I'd worked with the unit, Itchy had been the one to approach me asking questions about my background. He'd been in Street Crime forever. Sometimes when I saw him skulking around the precinct, the phrase "crazy military type" floated into my brain. Right now he was looking through a file of photos, perusing each one with a slight smirk on his face. "Seriously. Sacrilegious," he reprised after a downbeat.

"Fucking right," Toscano spit out, turning to face the table. "Fucking Asante."

No one had looked up when we'd walked in and sat in the two empty spots to Vic's right. They kept their eyes on whatever files they were looking at.

Vic had been training for about five years when I'd rolled into regular patrol, and he rolled into being the commander of Street Crime, where he seemed to find his mission in life. He'd shaped up the unit, and as a result more, better cops wanted to join. He was commanding a mix of these new hotshots and some old-school, permanent officers who'd been in Street Crime a long time.

"Fucking assholes," chimed in Toscano's partner, reaching for the photos Itchy had finished with.

"We gotta take those guys this time Sarge," Toscano punctuated his "gotta" with a pound on the old wood table.

Everyone but Itchy glanced up at Vic, but he was examining a file, pretending we weren't there. It felt like walking into an intimate family spat. And I was starting to get nervous about the assignment—it wasn't sounding like what I'd expected. At all.

Itchy's partner, Jack Willner, caught my eye and winked. I stared at him, not sure if the wink was friendly. Willner was the All-American boy-next-door type, tall and well-formed, nice to look at. His light brown hair was just right—styled, but not styled-looking. I felt rather than saw Chris turn to stare at him too. Willner averted his gaze to the diagram on the chalkboard in front of us.

I took the opportunity to look around. Other than the various costumes and props used for dressing up as johns and junkies for street-buys and jump-outs, nothing too different. Disappointed, I turned to study the chalkboard too.

I knew the history of the case. Everyone did. Asante Sarner was a break-off Vice Lord veteran and bad boy who thought he was now an independent businessman on the North Side. It seemed that whenever the Street Crime or Organized Crime units built up cases to bring him down, he dismantled operations and disappeared, only to show up a month or so later with an established operation in a new headquarters. He'd done that three times now, and Toscano wasn't the only one getting sick of it. Chris and I had heard about this new house, had driven by it earlier in the week. We'd seen the manger scene, complete with black Baby Jesus, Mary, and Joseph, which personally, I thought was pretty well done.

The chalkboard Willner was staring at had been downstairs a month ago, used by some internal Rembrandt who'd put a George H.W. Bush v Clinton poster up, modified so that Bush was saying, "Re-elect me if you don't want 'The First Black President.'" The sign hadn't lasted the next shift, but remnants of it framed the chalk diagram as if to mock those of us who might actually think of voting for a black president. Of course, we knew that would never happen.

The board showed a north Minneapolis city block with squares for houses complete with corresponding addresses. One house was circled, and an arrow pointed from it to a list on the left side of the board. Bullet points included the address and city-recorded ownership, one Edna Mae Williams, age 94, and continued, "Vice Lord involvement?" "Asante's new house?" and "Crew changes." This last item had a list of names under it. I recognized a couple of them.

While I waited my turn—that being last—for the photos and files, Vic finally either got sick of the belly-aching or got done reading. In any case, he snapped the last brown folder shut and tossed it to the guy on his left, who opened it and started paging through.

Vic referred to the Organized Crime unit. "Okay, so here's the deal. This is OC's operation, but they know they can't do it without us."

"Damn straights" and "Yeah, Sarges" filled the air.

Chris and I glanced at each other again, our earlier speculations about why we'd been invited to join obviously wrong. I felt a twinge in my stomach. Chris raised his eyebrows at me, and then went back to flipping mug shots.

After a minute, Vic pushed down as if on a pillow of air. The commotion ceased.

"Listen up. If we're going to get these guys this time, we need all of us. They're like fucking antelope, man. Got noses for us wolves from miles away. But they're as good as dead meat now."

Up with whoops and "fucking A's". Down with Vic's hands again on the air pillow.

"We're gonna need concentration on this one, men. Hear me. Willner, take your Ritalin and fucking pay attention. We are going to be on this fucking house twenty-four-seven through Christmas."

Groans and questions about overtime now filled the room, which Vic ignored as he continued. "Willner, you and Catfish are the new guys. We know they've never seen your faces, right?"

Nods all around.

"Okay, so we use you two for close-in work. OC wants us inside that house. So, Willner and Cat will be getting their suburban on, because we all know ain't no white boys getting in there without being scrubbed clean of cop." Looking over at them, he added, "You're going for liberal, rich, and uptown to even get close. Willner, that should come natural for you. Score a few times in a row, suggest you might have a market out in Maple Grove or Eden Prairie or wherever the fuck, see what that brings. We have to build this up fast. I want you two out there tonight. See if one of your street contacts can refer you in there. The rest of us will watch best we can in the vans, taking note of who and what's going in and out."

The first file of photos came to me, finally, and I flipped through. Of the twenty or more mug shots, I recognized two from street busts. Must be junior members of Asante's crew now, having proven themselves by doing the few months that repeated street charges brought.

"I'm thinking that plan has about a twenty-percent chance of working," Vic continued. "That's why Hausen and Quinby are here—our Plan B."

My stomach panged again, and just for a moment I thought I might throw up from nerves, right onto the unattractive mug of Jamal Jones, who I was pretty sure I'd popped when riding with Vic in the early days.

"Fresh fuckin' meat," Itchy murmured under his breath, shaking his head like it was a damn shame. Guess this wasn't going to be a your ordinary john round-up. All eyes were on me, so I went to work on my tough thing, looking up and meeting Vic's stare.

Vic moved his glare around the table. "Hausen joins us. Quinby'll be under with Bryce Davis."

That shut everybody up. Davis was a rising star among the brass. He'd been Raim's Field Training Officer at one time. He was one of the few black long-time cops on the MPD. And a fugg.

Chris knocked my knee with his under the table. I didn't react, but *Quinby'll be under* echoed in my head, causing the contents of my abdomen to agitate again.

Vic continued, "Davis is at some brass meeting, but he'll be by later. We'll meet with him in a couple hours. For now, listen the fuck up. This little gal was my rookie, and I know you know that. If anything happens to her, if she even gets her feelings hurt, I take it out of the hide of each and every one of you because it will take one of you fucking up to get her in harm's way, okay? Here's the deal. She and Hausen were chosen for this duty because of how they've performed on the street. They have better bust stats in uniform than you lazy mopes ever had in your miserable careers. And I think you all know Davis's record. These are cops, gentlemen, and you damn well better treat them like cops. Not rookies, not black or white or fucking men or women. Cops."

I looked around the table. They were staring. Most looked like they weren't sure of me, which didn't help with my stomach issues.

"Fuckin' A, man," said Willner. "She's kinda green for our type of work. Even if she is Hagen Quinby's niece or whatever."

Vic rose slowly to full height, fists on his hips.

Hagen Quinby was my uncle. My Dad's brother, the black sheep, and the only other member of the family in law enforcement. He was a Sergeant in the third precinct, but lots of guys had worked with him over the years, and if not, they'd heard of him.

Now the only one at the table standing, Vic glared at Mr. All-American. "Like I said, they were chosen because of how they've performed on the street."

Willner decided to push it. "Yeah, course Sarge. But c'mon, be honest. You need a woman, preferably one who's not blonde-blue, am I right?"

Time for me to pipe in. "Clear why he's on your squad, Sarge. Scary high IQ."

That got a snicker from Toscano and his partner, and a smirk from Itchy. Willner looked confused.

Toscano said, "Sarge, didn't Davis take Asante down the first time, 'bout a decade ago?"

Vic said, "Yeah. But Asante isn't actually in the house much, and it's been a decade. Davis can street-up like you wouldn't believe. With some extreme arm candy, they'll be distracted."

Nobody dared comment after Vic's little speech.

Toscano had another question. "What'd Asante do? A deuce?"

"Nah, whole nickel," said Vic. "Then two years in Chicago. He's been up our asses since."

Toscano nodded, then turned to Chris and me. "If we could get in there, get the layout of the rooms. Find where shit's kept, we might be able to get 'em before they flush or however they disappear things."

"OC's thinking exactly," said Vic, reminding us that our Fourth Precinct Street Crime unit was working with the department-wide Organized Crime unit. Then, turning to me and Chris, he said, "You up for it?"

"Hell, yeah," Chris said.

"Yeah, hell," I quipped.

. . . .

I DON'T LIKE IT, Kainda. I really don't like it."

"Yeah, I knew you wouldn't. I don't like it all that much. But it's a great opportunity for me and Chris."

We were lined up at The 21, our favorite after-shift hangout. I sipped a tap beer with a red daiquiri umbrella in it. Raim sat to my left, sipping his usual straight whiskey. Chris sat two down from Raim, with his wife Mandy between the two guys.

The umbrella was from Chris. On a trip the four of us took to Cancun the year before, Chris and I wrote a drunken partner-agreement on a cocktail napkin, signed it, rolled it up, and sealed it by running it through with daiquiri umbrellas. Ever since, we bought these umbrellas for each other at random times. I liked putting them on his seat in the squad, where he'd inevitably get poked in the ass.

The agreement, witnessed and signed by Raim and Mandy, read, "Together we protect and serve, in this we shall never swerve. We dearly love our Raim and Mandy, the two of them are sweet as candy." We'd thought it brilliant after about ten fruity rum drinks.

We'd been all talking earlier, but now Chris and Mandy leaned into each other, kissing and noogling, so Raim and I drifted into debriefing the day.

I'd met Raimondo Hannesen at eleven when he was sixteen, the same age as my oldest brother, who brought him home for dinner. We'd been together on and off since I was fifteen. Raim was respected by everyone he worked with because he worked hard. When something was on, he was like a dog with a bone. On stops, he'd search longer through cars for guns or drugs, occasionally coming up with something long after everyone else leaned against their squads bullshitting and telling stories. But he also played hard. Everyone loved him because he was fun, smart, and loyal.

Cop groupies and straight-women-rookies formed another kind of fan club. He was hot, but blessed with a certain amount of obliviousness to this fact. Five-ten, with a strong body, not overly bulked up. I think mostly it was the contrast of the dark brown curls and the blue eyes that did women in. Also, he was an amazing kisser. Performed related activities well, too. And I had high standards.

Last month, he'd let it slip after a Thanksgiving weekend evening in this same bar that he would propose to me over Christmas, but that he just loved me so much at that moment he couldn't wait. That probably had something to do with his sixth shot of whiskey, but I wasn't complaining. So we were "unofficially" engaged, with ring and announcement to come four days hence.

I was more nervous about this than I was letting on. Raim was trying to be a women's equality type, but it wasn't natural for him. His beloved Italian mother had stayed home to raise "her" four sons and gloried in it. Dad, a huge broad-shouldered second generation Dane, was an emotionally reserved retired cop. Two of Raim's brothers were married to women who just couldn't wait to get pregnant and stay home. I wasn't even sure I wanted kids, but I was sure I didn't want to stay home. The further our relationship went, the more I felt this issue press down.

Raim tilted this second shot of whiskey down his throat, clunked the glass on the bar, and took a long pull of beer. "I just want to know why every 'opportunity' you get seems to have to do with your body."

"Excuse me?"

"Oh come on, Kainda. You think you'd be asked to do this if you weren't drop-dead gorgeous? Weren't a part-something-not-white woman?"

I took a deep breath, staring at the door of the 1950s MPD cruiser that hung on the wall across the bar. Cop car doors from St. Paul and a few close-in suburbs surrounded it, but the old MPD door had the place of honor at The 21.

Working hard to keep my voice even, I said, "Thanks for the vote of confidence."

Raim signaled the bartender and another shot was poured. He stared at it and said, "I'm sure everyone involved with this knows why you're on it."

I looked from the cruiser door up to the ceiling. White Christmas lights were strung among lacy bras of every conceivable color and cup size nailed to the ceiling. They'd been "donated" by cop groupies who'd been talked out of them, mostly right here while they sat drinking. That didn't help my mood, so I looked back at the old MPD door for strength. To protect and serve.

I felt it rising—I was about to yell at Raim. I tried hard not to do that. I looked slowly around the bar. A group of Street Crime guys had come in and sat in the back. I caught Itchy's eye, and Willner looked like he'd just jerked his eyes away, studying something off in the distance. Toscano's eyes were on the ass of a woman walking by their table. I stared at Itchy. He shrugged almost imperceptibly and raised his glass to me. I picked mine up and sipped as I looked back at Raim.

The shot was gone, making three in an hour. Not a good sign. Not a good time to fight. That never stopped me though, not at twenty-four.

I looked at the MPD car door again and said softly, "I was selected for this assignment because my partner and I have the highest stats in our shift and because we like to get bad guys. You should know what that's like. You were the bad-guy-chaser in your shift your second year. No eating long, free Chinese meals for us. Not even fucking donut stops. We actually look for suspicious vehicles and that kinda shit. Sound familiar? Well, just be fucking glad you never had to work so fucking hard and then have people think you're picked for shit because you got a dick and balls." My voice rose though the tirade, but only to normal volume.

Chris had got up and was behind me, hand on my elbow. "Kainda, take a walk with me."

I shook his hand off.

"Raim," he said quietly.

"Fuck off, man," Raim said. "I don't get into your shit with your woman."

Chris held up both hands and headed back to his seat.

Turning to me, Raim said, "I hate it when you talk to me like that. Such a badass little cop, huh? Fine, have fun. Go wiggle your ass and flash your tits at that scum-sucking, baby-killing piece of shit. Just don't come back to my house afterwards."

He stood up, walked over to the door, swung it open, then paused. He stood there for a downbeat, then stepped out and slammed it shut behind him.

Tears stung behind my eyes, but they would not fall if I could help it. Not here.

Chris came around my other side and put his arm around me. Mandy slid down to Raim's barstool and laid her cheek on my shoulder. I was in a love sandwich.

"I need a minute, guys," I said. "Do me a favor?"

"Anything," Chris said.

"Deal with Raim? He's just had three shots in an hour and at least one beer."

"On it." Chris looked at Mandy and indicated the door with his head. Mandy squeezed my arm, got up, and put on her coat.

Chris leaned in. "You okay?"

I nodded. "Thanks."

He touched my shoulder, then moved his arm around Mandy. They headed toward the door.

I looked up and studied the bras. The lights did make beautiful shadows on the ceiling through the lace. The bartender set another beer next to my almost empty one.

"Thanks, John, but I'm done. I'll pay for it, but give it to someone who needs it."

He tilted his head to indicate behind me to the left. Itchy moved up and set his own glass, filled with amber liquid and ice, on the bar next to my fresh beer. He slid onto the newly vacant barstool, picked up his glass, and indicated a toast. I picked up mine.

Itchy clinked our glasses. "As the year dies."

I drank, gazing at him. I had no idea what he was talking about.

He said, "It's December 21st, Quinby. The old year dies with the sun, and the new sun is born. Tomorrow the day will be longer than today. A new year. But tonight, the old year dies."

His words were slurred. Great, all I needed was another heavy-drinking male cop right now. Nonetheless, the dark words seemed fitting, and I held up my glass for another clink, then drank.

"Hubby trouble?" he asked.

I grunted.

Failing in that line of conversation, he began singing to the tune of "Love in the Elevator," only the words were, "Going into Asante's."

Wonderful. Now I got to think about the assignment that pissed off Raim, and made me nervous. Toscano and Willner looked at us from across the bar. Toscano made a drinking motion with his empty hand to let me know Itchy'd had a few. I'd seen Itchy after he'd had a few before, but never close-up. I acknowledged the message, and decided to try to get Itchy talking. Maybe I'd learn something.

"You've been on Asante before. What should I be worried about?"

"Asante, Asante, Assholeante. Worry about every fuckin' thing, Hot One. He's gonna wanna bang you, he lays eyes on you."

"Davis can take care of that," I said.

"Yeah, I bet he can . . . ."

"That's not what . . . "

"I know, I know, Baby-Doll. Anyway, Raim ain't here to blow a gasket, is he? So, don't get your pretty little undies in a twist." He lifted his finger to signal he wanted another drink and made eye contact with the barkeep who, when Itchy looked away from him, looked over at Willner, who in turn looked at Toscano, who shook his head.

"Okay," Itchy continued. "Worry about the room in back with the huge TV that's on a constant loop of 'Blacks and Blondes.' Or, is it 'Blacks on Blondes'? Or, 'Blacks in Blondes.' Yeah, that's it. You ain't blonde. Oh no. But even so, they getcha in that room, you're fucked. Literally."

He laughed a maniacal laugh that got Toscano and Willner concerned again.

I widened my eyes at them. Help me out, guys.

I could almost see Toscano sigh. He got up, and Willner followed. They joined us, Toscano on my side, and Willner on Itchy's other side.

Willner laid a fist on Itchy's shoulder. "Itchy, man, you done for the night."

Itchy's " . . . the fuck," overlapped my, "Hey, I gotta run." I let them deal with him as I made my escape.

....

I WON'T SAY Raim and I completely made up, but we declared a temporary cease-fire with amazing sex that night. That was undoubtedly one of our problems.

Two nights later, Bryce Davis and I were undercover. He'd streeted-up so much even I didn't recognize him. He made himself out to be a player from Detroit, where he was originally from. I was his girl, and we did get in the house. They wanted us to party, which was tricky to get out of. As predicted, one room had a huge TV surrounded by obscene VCR-tape boxes showing many flavors of porn and acts that looked quite painful. We didn't see Asante Sarner, but his crew was much in evidence. I was blissed out on adrenaline the whole time, getting into the role after we got inside.

We conferenced with Organized Crime and Vic's unit afterwards, sketching out the main floor of the house. I'd got upstairs once to use the bathroom and had a sense of a couple of those rooms.

They were talking about whether they should raid immediately, or if we should try to get more, maybe off a wire. That's when I got my bad news. I wouldn't be involved in the operation any further. Too dangerous for a girl only a year-and-a-half in, and relatively new to undercover ops. But they let me attend all their meetings that evening and the next day. Gee, thanks.

At those meetings, something kept niggling at the corner of my mind, but I couldn't identify it. I concluded it was just how pissed I was at being cut out. The Organized Crime unit commander decided things were ripe for getting more information before the gang moved operations again. Plus, Asante wouldn't expect us on Christmas Day. Davis would wear a wire to get as much on tape as possible.

Raim volunteered for Christmas duty so he could get involved and the OT pay was sweet. And he probably wanted to avoid the whole engagement question. They'd use him on the perimeter with Chris. Perimeter duty was by seniority, so even there I was screwed.

So much for getting engaged on Christmas. Who knew if it would ever happen now? On Christmas Day, I moped around in bed as long as I could stand, and then went for a five-mile run in icy slush. At three p.m. I took a shower and tried to forget what was going down without me. Of course, that didn't work. I couldn't stop going over it.

Something was bugging me and I honestly couldn't tell if it was that I wasn't involved or something else.

I was rinsing lather from my hair when things fell together like the final pieces of a puzzle. I remembered a young informant—James, sometime last fall, telling me a rumor about some big gang banger talking up killing a cop in a set-up. It was going to make the guy a big man in the national gang with which he affiliated. I'd asked him to work it, but never heard more. Then again, I suspected James, a sweet kid not directly involved in gangs, of occasionally making stuff up to earn a few bucks, which he used to feed his grandmother.

And I remembered Itchy at The 21 talking about a huge TV and a specific type of porn.

I also remembered some things Toscano and Vic had said in our first meeting. Davis took Asante down the first time ten years ago. Asante did five years. Davis unrecognizable in his street garb. Asante prescient the last three times the cops had been ready to move on his operation. Toscano talked about Asante spending some years in Chicago, then coming back. Setting up a branch of a Chicago crew. A national gang?

I barely stopped to turn off the water. I jumped out of the shower and threw on the T-shirt and jeans I'd laid aside after doing some baking the day before, skipping nonessentials. I grabbed my revolver out of my gun belt in the bedroom, shoved it in my jeans pocket, dug out a second gun from my nightstand, shoved that in my thick sock, and ran out the door. I sprinted to my car, not thinking about anything but getting there.

I pulled up a block from the house. Just for an instant, I stopped. What if I was wrong?

I saw Raim staked out on the other side of the avenue and down a block, in a street outfit I'd seen before. I knew he was wired, listening to what was going on inside with Davis and Asante's crew. He stood with his finger to his ear. His stance, even at that distance, made me think something was already going wrong. I'd never forgive myself if I was too late. I flew out of the car and ran.

Raim's look of confusion deepened when he saw me and he signaled to someone I couldn't see. I glanced over for only a second, barely slowing. Concern intensified his face the moment he saw me. He started toward me. Then Chris came from around the corner. He was closer than Raim to me now. They glanced at each other, then Chris jogged toward me.

I pulled out my gun and held it up, knowing they'd pull theirs in response. Others on perimeter started to move, guys jumping from a couple of beat-up vans around the block. I shot up wide wooden porch steps and paused to push the cracked-open front door wider. I stepped in, knowing Chris wasn't far behind and Raim not far behind him.

The first room was completely empty except for a boom-box in one corner that was earning its moniker.

I was aware of my heart's quick beat as I inched forward toward an inner door frame with light streaming from it. I left the outside door behind me open.

There were rules in an operation like this. Breaking them could get someone killed. But this time, not doing something could also kill. I knew I could be wrong, but Davis's life was worth ruining a good wire op. At best, the op would bring down a big dealer and find out what else he was into. But as I'd realized in the shower, at worst, the whole thing was set up for a gang-initiation cop-killing.

Noises came from the next room.

"Do it," someone said.

I heard one boot stomp on the first wood porch step behind me. Chris. Then a shot.

I dashed into the brightly lit room. I was too late.

The world froze. I forgot to identify myself as police. Davis was bleeding onto grimy linoleum. Fury rose in me. Then I saw he was still alive and tried to keep my cool so I could keep him that way. His eyes tracked me. The banger in front to my right had his gun on Davis.

In the two seconds it took me to enter the room and assess what was going on, someone to my left yelled, "What the fuck!"

I knew that voice, but didn't take my eyes off the shooter.

I'd thrown on a T-shirt, I'd been wet, and it was about fifteen degrees out. I'm sure my nipples were evident under my shirt. Between that, the flour on my jeans, my partially lathered head, and the .357 I was pointing at the shooter's chest, I think I threw them off just long enough to give me time.

I looked at Davis on the ground and all I saw was Davis's little girl and Raim as a rookie looking up to Davis and Davis's fight for promotions.

In front of me, the shooter was looking to my left for direction. I looked into the shooter's eyes and saw yearning. In that moment I wasn't sure if it was for what he saw under my wet T-shirt or for killing a cop. A cop. To that asshole Davis was only a cop—a cop the killing of whom would make him a big man, someone to be respected.

In the slowest two seconds of my life, I watched the shooter's eyes and saw the moment he decided to finish off Davis. In the same instant, I fired my gun, growled, and rushed him. There was movement to my left. The shooter turned his weapon on me. I heard Chris's, then Raim's voices shouting, "Police! Freeze, fucking mother fuckers!"

The place exploded.

I was conscious of getting a second shot off, then of searing pain below my chin. Then I became aware of who I'd just heard. I'd known it, but it was so reprehensible I hadn't allowed it to register. I looked quickly to my left and pain burned hotter in my neck. A figure in dark clothes made for a narrow doorway. I knew the brown crew cut spiking out beneath the black stocking cap. Knew the wiry white neck. Knew the compact body and the way it moved.

Itchy.

I moved my left hand from the gun to my neck and held my gun one-handed, trained it on him. He turned his head. We locked eyes. I was aware of my hand on my neck, wet and hot. I pulled it away and looked. Thick red blood dripped from it. I put it back and looked at Itchy. Heavy brows rose and he bared two rows of gleaming white. My vision blurred, and I couldn't see him clearly, but I could see the smirk. Then, he was gone. Just as he disappeared, I felt myself fall. I heard Chris's strong voice. It seemed right in my ear.

"Kainda! No! Oh my god. You fu . . . ."

A blast blackened the world.

When I came to I was flat on my back. Raim's face was in mine, tears streaming from his blue eyes. It was completely silent and there were cops, in uniform and out, running everywhere. I looked up past Raim and saw the ceiling recede. I was in some kind of free fall and I couldn't breathe.

Rather than panic, my training kicked in and I concentrated on slowing everything down. Slow breath in, slow breath out. I felt a gurgling, like water in the small desktop fountain on the Precinct Commander's desk. He kept it there for serenity, he'd told me. Serenity. I relaxed every muscle to use less oxygen.

I closed my eyes and focused on slow breathing. When I opened them again, the ceiling was where it was supposed to be, and Raim's wet blue eyes were still there. I don't know if I smiled, but I felt I was smiling. His lips moved. I thought I could read them. "Hang on, Sugar Kain, hang on."

I tried to say, "It was Itchy," but something in my throat prevented it.

"Shhh, shhh, don't try to talk." Raim held my lower left jaw with his right hand.

I couldn't get a breath and the world slowed again. Raim turned his head and I was mesmerized by the curls in his hair. They were deep brown, but a light overhead made the curls glow red and gold. I watched his head and again read his lips, this time from the side, "Where the *fuck* is the ambulance?" Spittle flew in a glistening arc.

He turned to me again. Without moving the hand on my jaw, his other came up to my right cheek. He held my head and looked in my eyes.

Then he looked over next to me on the floor. I felt hot drips on my face—Raim's tears. I tried to turn my head that way, but he bent down and kissed my lips, hard. I felt the hot puffs of his breaths out as he sobbed. Then he lowered his ear to my mouth.

I had a flash of memory—me nibbling on that ear a couple months before, while we'd been watching a movie. Nibbling until he playfully but firmly threw me down on the couch and made love to me hard and fast, the movie forgotten. I wondered if this was what people thought about while dying—sex, love. I wished I'd gotten that damn ring. I wanted to get married, I suddenly realized, to Raim. Now. That made me cry.

Raim still looked at that spot past me. This time I turned my head to a searing pain on the left side of my neck. Chris lay there, a big hole in his chest. Oh Jesus God. I turned back to Raim, desperate. Tell me Chris is okay.

I read Raim's lips. "He saved your life. He saved your life."

Suddenly Vic's face appeared above Raim's. His hand rested on Raim's shoulder as he looked down at me. His mouth was a thin line. Was he really there, or was I imagining it? He'd been my protector for almost two years—was he here to save me now? Then he looked over at Chris. His lips trembled.

Other people in non-cop uniforms rushed in past me. Vic disappeared.

Then I heard him shouting, "Don't bother with that fucking asshole. Save these three . . . ."

I heard a droning response and Vic's voice yelled, "Do it. Now!"

Then other people surrounded me and I watched their faces, features marred with concern. I wondered again if I was going to die and I made a deal with God. I agreed to go if Davis and Chris could stay. I don't have kids, I told God, so it's only fair to take me. I felt calm after that.

I had a vague sense of needles entering my arm. Raim's face appeared again, but then as I stared into his eyes, his face floated away from me. I was in free fall again.

I amended my deal with God. I needed to tell Raim one more thing. I looked at Raim intensely to get his attention. Hearing was coming back. Someone shouted, "Get me an airway here."

Raim was floating away, but I finally got him with my stare. He came close again. I tried to talk, but nothing came out. I felt that gurgling again. Raim moved back to try to read my lips. I said, "Itchy. It was Itchy. I couldn't shoot him. And, Raim, they'll know. James." I named my young informant. "Get him off the streets. Please."

He nodded and touched my cheek with the palm of his hand. His face was a mess, eyes and nose streaming. I'd never seen him like that. He turned away to talk to someone and the face of the EMT took his place. I felt a sharp pain in my throat and at the same time the drug kicked in and the world faded to black.

. . . .

I QUIT.

After I got shot, during the investigation of what I'd done, I quit and went back to grad school. I gave up rebelling against my parents and went to business school.

I knew I'd fucked up the shooting. Two ex-Lords were dead. Davis lived, but Chris was gone. Little CJ was fatherless and Mandy a widow.

They said I'd saved Davis's life, but in my mind, I'd killed Chris. He died backing me up—saving me—as the year died.

Itchy disappeared and Asante's crew didn't reemerge for over a year. But they reemerged, so it was for nothing.

Davis recovered and is now the assistant chief. A good, solid cop. A stand up guy. A role model. A father. His little girl is in college now, and has a little brother.

I broke up with Raim not long after the shooting. I was wrecked, and so was he. He wanted to take care of me. Although I couldn't imagine my life without him, I also knew I wasn't what he needed. Not how I was after Chris died. Probably not before either. I could see what being with me was doing to him.

He made lieutenant several years ago and from what I hear he's the best investigator the MPD has ever had—even getting national attention.

I was still bed-ridden when they buried my partner, but Mandy came to consult me about Chris's service and gravestone. A few weeks later, although I still had my trach and it was cold and snowy out, I walked with Mandy to Chris's grave. I needed to see it, to see the Shakespeare she'd asked me to approve. It was perfect. The entire MPD had chipped in a few dollars each for a huge stone and the inscription Mandy wanted. It said:

~

Christopher H. Hausen
Father of Chris Junior
Husband of Miranda
Brother, Son, Friend, Cop
Lost in the line of duty
Minneapolis Police Department
December 25, 1991

~

Cowards die many times before their deaths;
The valiant never taste of death but once.

~

Mandy and I keep flowers on it at all times. And every year at Christmas, I leave a hand-written copy of our partnership agreement, speared in the snow with a red daiquiri umbrella.

T. J. Roth lives in Minneapolis. She is the author of numerous published articles and book chapters, but this is her first fiction publication. She has completed one unpublished book featuring Kainda Quinby, *Murder by Degree,* and is working on the second, *Suicide by Cop*. Both are set in present-day Minneapolis. She thanks the MPD, especially Captain C. Leaf and Sergeant D. Smulski, Jr. and his 2004-05 Third Precinct CRT Directed Patrol.

A Visit From Santa

Marlene Chabot

Not a creature was stirring, not even a mouse." The brunette with bright blue eyes interrupted her reading of Clement C. Moore's famous Christmas poem so she could tuck the soft, blue woolen blanket under her son's chin; the tyke was losing his battle with the sandman.

Four-year-old Chris took advantage of his mother's silence. "Mommy, what does *stirring* mean?"

"Well," Mary Knox replied in a hushed tone, "Remember the big spoon we used to help us make Christmas cookies today?"

"Uh huh."

"The spoon helped move the eggs, flour and sugar into one big lump." The young mother moved her arm like she was mixing something with a spoon. "We stirred the ingredients together."

The little boy turned on his side and sighed.

Mary leaned over her sleepy son, kissed him tenderly on the forehead and said, "I think it's time to close your eyes young man so Santa can come."

"Santa won't put coal in my stocking, will he?"

"I don't think so. You've been a good boy for Mommy and Daddy."

Chris grinned and finally permitted his eyes to close.

As Mary quietly shut the door to her son's room behind her, she heard several loud clunks coming from the floor below. Apprehensive, she took a deep breath and tried to think logically and remain calm. She was not a child, and no one was trying to break into her home. At least, not again. More than likely the noise she heard was caused by the old plumbing system or the furnace which had been giving them problems lately. Minnesota's cold winters were notorious for being hard on both plumbing and heating.

The young mother listened for more sounds but nothing came. Luckily she recalled what she had done right before she came upstairs with her son. "It's the dishwasher," she said in a whisper, "just going through its cycles." She continued across the hall and into the master bedroom where all the unwrapped Christmas presents were still waiting for her.

Now that Mary was surrounded by packages of every shape and size, she desperately tried to get into the spirit of the holiday, even though her hubby, a Delta Airlines pilot, was stranded on the east coast due to a snowstorm. As she pulled colorful ribbons and decorated paper out of their separate containers and matched them up with each gift, she began to hum her favorite childhood Christmas song, *Twelve days of Christmas*.

After each item was carefully encased in paper and decked out with a bow, Mary stacked the gifts neatly on the floor by the bedroom door where they would sit until she was ready to carry them downstairs and set them under the Christmas tree.

Three hours passed by before Mary secured the last bow in place. As she stood now and stretched her tall thin frame, she quickly glanced at the clock-radio by the bedside. It was eleven-thirty. No wonder she was so tired. She usually went to bed around ten. Since it was so late, she decided to change into her flannel pajamas before she made the necessary trips downstairs with the many gifts.

Just as she started to unbutton her cotton blouse she heard weird noises like before. *No dishwasher runs that long.* Goose bumps quickly covered her arms and legs and she shivered.

"It's nothing," Mary bravely told herself as she tried to brush her fears away. "It's only natural to hear strange sounds in an old house like ours." But as much as she tried to convince herself everything was okay, she couldn't get the image of a certain terrible man out of her mind. He had been haunting her ever since he broke into her parent's house when she was only seven.

The big bald man with jagged scars slashed across his face was a mean drunk. He pushed everybody around, including her. She heard he had been in and out of jail many times since breaking into her childhood home. Could he be on the lam now? Does he still want to get even with her or another family member? Mary's fears wouldn't subside. "I wish Ryan were here. He always knows how to help me through my bad memories."

But Ryan wasn't here to offer assistance. Tonight, Mary knew she'd have to get through whatever was happening on her own. She inhaled deeply and waited. Nothing. "I can't stay in this bedroom forever. I've got to go downstairs."

Mary tiptoed to her bedroom door now and locked it before she continued to get ready for bed. As soon as her pajamas were on, she slipped into her thick pink fleece bathrobe. Then she strolled over to the bed to pick up the only object in the room she felt would offer some sort of defense, and stashed it in a pocket of her bathrobe. If there's a prowler in my house, at least I can lash out at them with the scissors, she thought.

Feeling prepared for survival, the young woman plucked up her first stack of presents, cracked the bedroom door and listened. But there was nothing to hear but deep silence.

She entered the dark hallway and slowly descended the dimly lit carpeted staircase. Each time her feet moved to the next step her eyes searched the area below for any evidence of an intruder before she allowed herself to continue on. So far everything in this part of the house appeared to be in its proper place. But what about the other rooms I can't see, she wondered?

After all the presents had finally been stashed under the Christmas tree, Mary decided to do a thorough search of the house. Nothing seemed to be disturbed. All the doors and windows were locked securely. "See," Mary said softly to herself as she made her way back to her bedroom, "you let your imagination run wild again. Now get to bed."

At five o'clock in the morning, Mary was awakened by loud screams. Her thoughts immediately went to her son who shouts in his sleep when he's having nightmares. She got out of bed to check on Chris, and indeed the boy was sleeping soundly. Mary scrambled back to her bedroom and threw on her bathrobe. She checked to make sure the scissors were still in her pocket. Just in case.

When she reached the entryway, she found the front door wide open. This time she was certain someone had entered the house. Bears are hibernating this time of year, and smaller animals can't get through a storm door and a wooden door too.

Mary's thoughts immediately raced to the presents under the Christmas tree as she spun in the direction of the living room. It was lit up like a baseball field. And there in the middle of the room, quietly minding his own business, was the jolly old man himself. He was sitting in the maple rocker that once belonged to her great-grandma. Resting on the floor next to his shiny black-booted feet was a huge bag filled to the brim. "What's going on in here?" Mary cried out as she cautiously made her way to where Santa sat.

Santa didn't answer.

The anxious brunette left a good six feet of space between herself and the red-suited visitor. There was no way he was getting near her. "What do you want?"

"Hey, you should try these Christmas cookies," a gentle man's voice said from behind Mary.

She whipped around and found another Santa. "What...? What's going on? Who are you?" she demanded. "Why are you here?"

"I'm here because I want to be, Mary," the second Santa said. "Where's my glass of milk?"

Caught off-guard by such an absurd request, Mary just barely managed to say, "Sorry, I forgot."

The Santa standing next to Mary was in no hurry to join the other Santa in the living room. His hazel eyes stared at her face briefly, "You don't have any idea who I am, do you?"

She shook her head from side to side.

"Honey, don't be afraid. It's only me."

Mary tugged on the snow white beard that was speckled with cookie crumbs. "Ryan. You made it home after all." Relieved, Mary threw her arms around her husband. "So who's the man in the rocking chair?"

"Oh," Ryan said nonchalantly, "the next door neighbor hired him to deliver their kids presents."

The other Santa finally opened his mouth. "I lost their house number and all I remembered was that they were leaving the front door open for me. So when I saw your door open, I thought I'd found the right house. Sorry I scared your husband, lady."

Just then the door to Christopher's room opened and a little voice said, "Mommy."

Mary swiftly focused her eyes on her husband again. "Quick, go in the kitchen and take that Santa outfit off." Once Ryan disappeared, Mary answered her son. "I'm downstairs Chris. Come and see who's here."

Chris screamed when he saw Santa sitting in the rocking chair. "Mommy, Mommy it's Santa. He stopped for a visit."

"That's right, Chris," Santa replied as he lifted the boy on his lap. "Now what was it you wanted for Christmas."

"I wanted my daddy."

Santa snapped his fingers. "Your wish is granted. You'll find him in the kitchen." Then Santa set the little boy down, picked up his black bag and waltzed out the door.

Marlene Chabot a native Minnesotan, received a B.S. degree in education from St. Cloud State University, an A.A.S. in business/marketing from Anoka Ramsey Community College and has also earned a writer's certificate from the Institute for Children's Literature. The author has been writing articles for Her Voices, a quarterly magazine of the Brainerd Dispatch, since 2007. She has also been published in the Brainerd Dispatch and the magazine *Central Minnesota Women*. She is a member of Sisters in Crime and the Great River Writers. Marlene started writing mysteries in 1995 and has just completed her third Minnesota based PI novel.